Lulu Jingle
By Jim Atkisson

Copyright
2024

A Toy Making Gadget Called the "Gizmo 3000"

My name is Howard, and this is a story about a clumsy, energetic elf named Lulu Jingle, but before I really get into Lulu's story, I have to bring you up to speed with Elf life, and our life here at the North Pole.

Not all elves build toys. *I know, shocker isn't it?* I think it's a little misconception among people in the Lower Latitudes, *"All elves must build toys..."*

I'm sure you're thinking, *"What are the Lower Latitudes?"*

That's a great question! The Lower Latitudes are anywhere, south of the North Pole. This is where Santa delivers toys on every Christmas Eve, but back to Lulu Jingle' story.

Not all Elves were born with the same talents and gifts. Some elves were born to be natural bakers. Other elves are just natural at being merry! Don't get me wrong, *all* elves are merry, and full of Christmas Cheer, but there are just *some* who are higher on the Christmas Cheer Spectrum and take it to another level. There are elves who are quite handy working in our North Pole Public Works Department. The North Pole Public Works Department is very busy taking care of the grounds around Santa's Castle, the factories and keeping our roads plowed. It's a thankless job, keeping those roads plowed, because without our roads, operations around Santa's Workshop and the many factories up here in the North Pole would just simply shut down. Can you imagine trying to move tons of toys to Santa's sleigh from their factory of origin in ten foot snow drifts? Speaking of Santa's Sleigh, there are elves who maintain the sleigh and care for his reindeer. We have elves who keep up with the fleet of trucks, tractors, and wagons as well.

We have rush hour up here and we get traffic and weather reports from our only radio station. WKO-KLAUS is our radio station, and they play a lovely mix of Christmas Carols.

We also have a clandestine special ops team. Those elves are agents, agents who serve down there in the Lower Latitudes, and keep up the surveillance on those nice, and naughty kids. I'll be honest, I've never met any elf on those special ops teams, because they rarely make it back up to the North Pole. They have a direct line to Santa's office.

The North Pole runs like a finely tuned machine. There's a delicate balance when it comes to the division of labor among elf culture. Every elf has purpose, a place, and a job. However, there are some notable exceptions. There are *those* who need a little help from Santa to find a place for them. We have a tremendous responsibility and a very tight window of time to get our jobs done. Once a year, we deliver toys to all the good boys and girls, and believe me, that's a tall order, with a very small margin of error. We need all elves to perform their jobs, but on occasion, there are some elves who don't fit the mold.

Early on, elves are tested to see what their particular attitudes are. Santa is our conductor and elves are the orchestra. On Christmas Eve, Santa's sleigh is packed tight with that year's toys and we send him out on his way towards the Lower Latitudes. We only pause long enough to wave *Goodbye* to Jolly Ole St. Nick, and before we've lost sight of his twinkling sleigh lights, we ramp up for the next Christmas Eve! We're very busy up here!

On the rare occasion when we have an elf who never seems to fit in any of the more traditional roles we have, Santa has to get creative, because like I said...*all elves have purpose here in the North Pole.*

It's sad to watch an elf flounder around until Santa finds a role for them. Believe it or not, for example, we have some elves who have an allergy to Reindeer, but despite this sensitivity, there's a place for them in Santa's Castle. Those elves are quite happy masquerading in the Lower Latitudes as Christmas bell ringers and will act as Santa's Liaison with some key officials down there when they're not masquerading as those cheerful Christmas bell ringers. I'm proud to say, we've never lost an elf!

Thinking back, it's been awhile since we had an elf who needed Santa's help finding their way and purpose. Before Lulu Jingle, the very last elf who needed Santa's direct involvement was Stanley Dumbroski. As you can imagine, we have lots of chimneys up here in the North Pole. We have houses, stores, factories, taverns, and several theaters, and since we live in a city where it snows...every day...we have many fireplaces.

In the spirit of full disclosure; I'll share a little known fact about elves...*we prefer warmth and sunshine.*

We have sunny days here in the North Pole, and the sun is very intense, but it never gets warm enough for us. It's always bitter cold, and if we're being honest, elves simply don't like cold, and if we had it our way, we'd all move to Palm Springs or Phoenix, but our purpose is here, and our work is by nature top secret.

We have to remain hidden, and our workshop is top secret. No one knows where Santa Castle is, or his Workshop. Our city is hidden, our way of life remains a mystery, and very few people have actually met Santa Claus. The only place we can maintain this level of secrecy is *at* the North Pole.

So we're stuck here at the North Pole and we live in a city with endless chimneys and fireplaces. One day, along comes Stanley Dumbroski. Dumbroski is a jolly enough elf, but he's a tad slow on the manufacturing line. You see, elves are right handed, and Stanley Dumbroski is a leftie and struggled in a right handed world, especially on the production line. Dumbroski is allergic to Reindeer, can't carry a tune, and burns toast, so working in the bakery division wasn't a good fit for him. Though he's a jolly, happy elf, he just didn't score high enough on the jolly-aptitude test to find a spot within the full time Jolly Elf Division. Suffice, this presented a challenge for Santa Claus and he really had to think. It seemed there was little hope for Stanley Dumbroski, but like I say, Santa has never lost an elf. Santa realized there are an endless number of chimney's here at the North Pole, and although we'd never experienced one fire at the North Pole, we suddenly needed a North Pole Chimney Sweeping Division, and Dumbroski would be the lead in the new division. Turns out Stanley Dumbroski was a natural at cleaning chimneys and can be heard caroling and singing high on rooftops, and though he can't carry a tune, or melody, he sounds so jolly and cheerful as he sweeps our chimneys clean.

I'll share another, previously guarded secret of the North Pole. *Not all of the toys that Santa delivers to the good boys and girls are made here in the North Pole!* I can understand why that is a shocking revelation and the only reason why I'm at liberty to share this, it was only recently declassified. This was a huge secret, and the only more guarded secret, is the precise location of our city here at the North Pole. The North Pole is a big, desolate place, but aside from Jay Edgar Hoover and the understanding he had with Santa, no one knows where our city is. The only reason why the director of the FBI never spilled the beans to the United States Congress about what he knew about Santa's Castle and the other intel he knew about life at the North Pole...Santa Claus threatened Jay Edgar Hoover with the list. The naughty list, and the Director didn't want to find himself on the naughty list on Christmas Eve. So the Director of the FBI never gave up the secret of Santa's Castle.

So with that said, there's been a Christmas season, or two when we didn't come close to meeting our quota of toys and Santa had to turn to outside help. Some years there were an exceptional number of boys and girls on the nice list. You see, every year we have our "nice kids" numbers baked into our projected toy quota. This data is gathered by those elves in the special ops teams and passed onto Santa, and this combined with the previous years numbers, and with the current birth rate in the Lower Latitudes we're able to project how many toys we're going to need for that given year on Christmas Eve. We have a three point margin of error, plus or minus, but overall we're pretty spot on with how many toys we need for Santa. Some years, the boys and girls just break our analytics and we run short on toys. Believe me, it's a good problem for us to run into, and it makes the boss very happy when we have more nice boys and girls than we have toys. Santa knows by Black Friday if we're going to have enough toys on hand and if we run short, he has to turn to outside vendors to fill the gaps.

One thing you should know about Santa Claus, he never forgets his friends. During the Second World War we ran into a crisis and we couldn't keep up with the unexpected demand during the Christmas of 1941. It was during the Christmas rush of 1941 Santa Claus asked help from Giuseppe's Toy Emporium. Did I say, Santa never forgets his friends, because Salvador Giuseppe was a friend of Santa Claus.

Wow! Can you imagine such a thing, to be known as a close personal friend to Santa Claus?

Talk about having connections in life, if you have Santa's direct phone number to his office. I mean, we have such reverence for Santa, so much so whenever we speak his name, there's a temptation to almost whisper his name, but Santa is so jolly and cheerful he wouldn't want that. Even Jay Edgar Hoover, the notorious director of the FBI, was nervous about crossing Santa Claus, so much so he pleaded the 5th Amendment when the United States Congress insisted he give up the location of Santa's Castle, and his workshop. In all fairness, Mr. Hoover got extra in his Christmas Stocking for his unwillingness to cooperate with congress during their depositions and hearings regarding the central question, "Is there actually a Santa Claus?"

Personally, I can't imagine the sort of conversation, or the surprise on Mr. Giuseppe's face when Santa knocked on his front door that day after Thanksgiving in 1941. I'd like to imagine it, but I'm sure my imagination won't do it any justice. I'm sure Salvador Giuseppe was delighted, and surprised. I heard when Santa travels in the Lower Latitudes during the off season, he rides in a very long, black sedan. He appears very business-like. A sharp, and impeccable dresser. Always in a three piece suit and shiny shoes. If you happen to see Santa Claus in the Lower Latitudes during off season, you won't find him wearing *the suit*. I would be remiss if I didn't admit I wish I were a fly on the wall during that legendary moment. That moment when Santa reached out to someone in the Lower Latitudes for help. We simply couldn't hope to meet the demand that season, because Santa waved requirements for any kid to be on the Nice List. There was no Naughty List during World War Two. Santa was grieved for the children of the world and wanted to do his part to support the kids, and bring any light during a global conflagration like World War Two.

It was early in the war and the United States just declared war on darkness, and Santa felt it was time to ask for help. Until nations were at peace with one another again, Santa deemed that no child would go without a toy under the tree, or in their stocking...no matter how bad they'd been that year. After the war, Santa waited a couple of years before rolling back out the Naughty List.

Mr. Giuseppe was a legend when it came to building toys. A few of us were convinced he was a distant relative of Santa Claus, because few in the Lower Latitudes could build toys like the elves in Santa's Workshop. He would turn out toys around the clock, with little break. He was passionate about toys and that showed in his toy store in Manhattan, New York City. Salvador Giuseppe never received compensation for his work during those years, and went unnoticed by anyone in the Lower Latitudes. He would often neglect his own business to help Santa's need to help children globally during the war. If it weren't for him, and his tireless effort, our workshops and factories could never have met those projections each Christmas Eve.

I have to say it again, because it's important to Lulu Jingle's personal story. Santa never forgets his friends, and he was personally grateful to Salvador. Santa told Mr. Giuseppe if he ever needed anything, to please let him know. Well, as the story goes at the time, Salvador Giuseppe was a proud man, and never asked for help from Santa Claus. Even during deep economic recessions, he never called in any favors to his friend up at the North Pole. Though he had his phone number, a direct line to Santa's personal office in his castle, Salvador Giuseppe was always sincere in his help with Santa during the war.

Eventually as time passed, and the Second World War became a distant history, and people seemed to forget the lessons of the war, and global commerce changed, we lost our friend Salvador Giuseppe. The toy maker had lived a full life, and passed away at the ripe age of Ninety-Seven. He worked well into his eighties from what Santa learned when he went to pay his respects, and of course he was dressed in one of his charcoal colored suits, and leaving his famous red coat and hat at home, no one seemed to recognize it was Old St. Nick paying his respects.

Mr. Giuseppe left the Toy Emporium to his daughter, and though she loved toys, and her father's legacy, the economy had changed. The way consumers purchased toys for their children was different after Mr. Giuseppe passed. The change had been in the wind for many years, but Salvador was unwilling to imagine a world where parents no longer visited their local toy stores.

Though Giuseppe's Toy Emporium was nicely situated across the street from Central Park in New York City, customers were less frequent to come over to his side of the street to browse his shelves. It seemed customers were more interested in shopping online, or visiting large box retailers, instead of a locally owned toy store. The romance of browsing his shelves, wasn't what it used to be. Christmas is a special time around New York City, and Giuseppe's Toy Emporium was a jewel in the city during Christmas. Florida Giuseppe urged her father to adapt to the new ways of commerce and open an online toy store and ship his toys to customers online, but the Master Craftsman of Fine Toys refused to change. He believed the magic of toys came from visiting a toy store, and allowing a child's imagination to wander the shelves, and explore the endless ways a toy could tell a story and express a boy, or girl's unique story by playing with toys. Over the years, his business would just decline, and Santa's good friend suffered with the loss of business. The toy store's prospects looked grim as time went on. Salvador Giuseppe refused to surrender the idea of a toy store, because he remembered the glory years of toys and toy store shopping.

Whenever Santa Claus stopped in to check in on his friend, his heart would break for his friend. Santa Claus is a gentleman and would never try to force his help on his genius, but stubborn friend. We all sat helplessly from the sidelines of the North Pole and watched the decline over the years.

There was something very magical about Giuseppe's Toy Emporium during the Christmas season. The tree was always brightly lit at Rockefeller Center, and snow was a regular occurrence in New York City, and a White Christmas was always a possibility. There was a famous Thanksgiving Day Parade to kick off the Christmas season, and festive Christmas Carolers could be heard singing joyful Christmas Carols around Central Park. Bell Ringers could be heard wishing a passerby, *"Merry Christmas!"* as they tossed spare change into their buckets. Department stores were dressed for the season, with grand window displays. Radio City Hall always had a Christmas Musical on stage, and the overall vibe in the city was a festive one during Christmas.

If you were fortunate to stop off at Giuseppe's Toy Emporium during the season, you were always treated to a complimentary cup of Hot Chocolate. There was a table with Christmas Cookies, and other yummy pastries, and all complimentary. The store smelled like Pine trees, vanilla extract and maybe Cinnamon, but whatever the smell was, it just smelled like Christmas in Giuseppe's Toy Emporium. Local New Yorkers were all very familiar with Giuseppe's Toy Emporium and, because the toys were all affordable, and high quality craftsmanship, families traveled from all five boroughs to shop. Tourists heard by word of mouth, or were just lucky to come across the famous toy store while visiting the *Big Apple.*

There was magic in this little store, and it's why Santa turned to Salvador during the war. Once inside of his store, visitors *always* felt they'd experienced the North Pole, and perhaps Santa's Workshop.

Sorry, sorry for the laugh, if those customers only knew why they'd felt they'd been to the North Pole, well only you and I know it's because Santa visited the store from time to time to visit his friend.

It *did* sound like the North Pole inside of Giuseppe's Toy Emporium, because Christmas Carols played all the time, customers were delighted and laughed with Salvador as he regaled visitors with cheerful banter. All were welcomed, even if no one purchased a toy. Salvador loved New York, and his Toy Emporium imbibed the very nature of Jolly Old Saint Nick. There was garland, and holly dangling from the rafters and ceiling, and so as to not be outdone by Macy's, Saks Fifth Avenue, or the other large department stores in Manhattan there was always a new window display out front, to showcase his latest toys. This was his passion, greeting people, making children happy, crafting new toys, and representing his city to tourists from all over the world. He greeted everyone with a jolly, "Merry Christmas!" He treated everyone as a friend, even if they'd only met for the first time. Even outside of his store, Salvador Giuseppe had a good heart, and was kind to everyone he met. He often told his family he was in a unique position, and an emissary of goodwill.

With all that said, it's natural to understand why Santa treated Mr. Giuseppe as a close personal friend. It's been said, Salvador Giuseppe was the only person living in the Lower Latitudes to have an open invitation to our city and Santa's Castle. The two men had a close bond and Santa had a personal interest in the success of Giuseppe's Toy Emporium.

When Florida Giuseppe felt compelled to surrender, and sell off the store to a local Manhattan Developer, it was a hard day for Santa Claus. It was the second blow to Santa, the first was when he heard his dear friend had passed away peacefully in his sleep. In fact, it appeared all would be lost, until one bright morning, Santa looked out from his window and saw a familiar, peculiar elf falling down another hill.

Lulu Jingle was one of those few elves who never fit the mold into what is known as Elf Life. *Lulu Jingle marches to her own drum.* She is head and shoulders above most elves when it comes to merriment, and Christmas Cheer, so much so, it makes her somewhat of a liability here in the North Pole. *She's very clumsy, and accident prone.* In all fairness, what she lacks for in grace, Lulu makes up for in speed. Lulu Jingle is the fastest toy maker on record. Too bad, she's all thumbs, because she's lightning fast when it comes to the "Gizmo 3000" and could turn out an entire zip code's worth of toys in fifteen minutes, and do it flawlessly, right down to the toy's specs.

...What's the Gizmo 3000? Of course, silly me, good question. The Gizmo for lack of a better term, is nothing more than a sophisticated toy making gadget. Now, I will say, the Gizmo 3000 actually has a different name, Gizmo is just a nickname we gave it, because none of us know what to call it. For security reasons, the higher ups keep the name of the Gizmo 3000 tight-lipped. Now, I will say we're on a third generation Gizmo.

It works under a simple premise. We enter the blueprint for a toy, any toy, and in a few moments, out comes the toy. Now, it takes a steady hand to work the 3000, because it can act up, and behave like a bucking bronco at a rodeo. The more toys you make, the more the 3000 jumps, and jolts and bangs, and shoots toys out onto the production line. They're noisy and create organized chaos as they work to build toys. Don't ask me how they actually go about making toys, they just *do.* Perhaps they use a little North Pole magic, but they just make toys, lots of toys, especially in the right elf hands.

When you use them, you really have to keep an eye on them and not get distracted, because they can go off the rails, and explode into a cloud of tinsel dust. Poor Lulu Jingle has been through more Gizmo 3000's than any other elf, because the 3000 met its match in Lulu Jingle and it tries to outwork her ability to make toys and before you know it, poof, another cloud of tinsel dust.

But, when Lulu slows down, and lets the Gizmo 3000 work the way it was designed, it's impressive to watch the amount of toys the pair can build together, but Lulu gets in her own way, and before you know it, another cloud of tinsel dust in manufacturing.

It was Black Friday when Santa looked out his office window and thought of a plan to reduce his friends down in New York City. Jolly Ole Saint Nick laughed one of those deep, belly laughs he's known for, and with a bright twinkle in his eye, he dashed off to his wall safe and spun the dial of the safe's lock. In no time, Santa pulled out a dusty blueprint and brushed it off. Santa, the master of all toy makers, had to replicate himself so the elves could build toys as fast as Santa does. Santa was the original toy maker, until it got to be too much, because he had to keep up with the whole operation in the North Pole by himself, so he reached out to his neighbors, the elves. We were once neighbors, and were feeling a little discontented with the North Pole, and were considering a move south to the Lower Latitudes. Santa presented us an offer to work together to bring joy to children worldwide, and before you know it, we accepted and moved over to his side of the North Pole, and built a city around his Workshop, and Castle. Santa had to teach us how to make toys, and though we were eager to learn, we couldn't match *Santa Claus*, and so he crafted the Gizmo 1000 to help us build those toys.

Over the years Santa had to refine the Gizmo, and introduce a new model to keep up demand. We transitioned from the 1000, to the 2000 model a few years before I came on staff. The 2000 was a good model, but the Gizmo 3000 was by far, more superior, and it was a good fit for the elves to build toys for Santa, but that was until Lulu Jingle. We're not sure what makes the Gizmo go, but all we know, it's meant to match Santa's toy making skills, and when one model blows, it turns into tinsel dust. Santa keeps the blueprints to all models in his wall safe, and no elf has ever seen those blue prints.

Santa has connections all over the world, among US Presidents, Jay Edgar Hoover, leaders in business, and one important ad agency boss. This very influential ad executive owed Santa a favor, because he begged to have his name removed from the Naughty List one year, and Santa agreed to extend grace, just that once, but the ad executive was so grateful, he told Santa if he ever needed anything, and I mean anything, to call him! Santa had a plan, his eyes were twinkling as he gazed at the blueprints for the Gizmo 4000.

That's the backstory, the backstory of how an overly energetic, silly hearted elf changed the outcome for one special toy store in New York City. The wheels were in motion to sell the toy store. The papers were to be drafted, and it was *supposed* to be the toy store's last Christmas season. It was Black Friday, and the lawyers were out for the holidays, and they felt it would be good to wait until January 1st to liquidate, you know, have a Merry Christmas, see you in the New Year. The developers were vultures, and eager to swoop down on Giuseppe's Toy Emporium.

After Santa made the phone call to Wiggins of New York Ad Agency, he went to work to craft and build the Gizmo 4000. The 4000 never made it to testing, the engineers said it wouldn't work. No elf alive could manage the speed of the Gizmo 4000 and it would blow big time, and spread tinsel dust all over the North Pole. They shook their heads at Santa, and said, "It can't be done!"

Santa Claus knew differently, and he knew one elf who could take his Gizmo 4000 and help his friends in New York. Santa went back to his office window and flung the frost covered window, and with a big, jolly, "Ho!Ho!" He called in a loud voice for Lulu Jingle.

Florida Giuseppe

Florida Giuseppe watched with a heavy heart from her store's window as potential shoppers passed her store, without so much as a pause, or consideration for what her store might have to offer in the way of a new toy. Florida was about to turn over her "Open" sign to *Sorry we're Closed* when she heard her phone abruptly ring. It startled her for a moment. The phone rang again, as she stared at, confused, and uncertain as to why, anyone would *actually* call her Toy Emporium anymore.

"Mom! Are you going to answer it?" Florida's daughter asked from the back of the store.

The phone rang again. She didn't want to get her hopes up. She wasn't her father. Salvador Giuseppe would never have surrendered his store, but times were different.

"It's probably a wrong number," Florida said glumly. No one calls her store. Everything is online these days. They're strolling right past her front door, but no one is remotely curious to stop in, and browse her inventory. Her father taught her how to make toys, and like Salvador Giuseppe, Florida had a passion for toys, but she was also a realist, and it was simply...*over.*

She had a mountain of invoices coming due again, and now she was out of cash. The cash her father had squirreled away during the good times. The store, and everything they had would have to be liquidated to avoid bankruptcy.

"Mom!" her slightly annoyed teenager yelled from the back stockroom. Autumn Giuseppe was helping out after school with inventory.

"You get it Autumn. I'm busy," Florida said as she walked away from the persistent phone caller.

"Busy doing what mom? Turning off the 'Open for Business' sign?"

"Stop. I'm sure it's a debt collector, why else would they keep calling?"

"I apologize mom, I'll get it before they hang up," Autumn said as she jogged up front to grab the ringing telephone.

"Merry Christmas, and thank you for calling Giuseppe's Toy Emporium, how can we help you?"

There was a brief pause in the conversation as Florida, half listened. She watched the bustling sidewalk. The city was already alive with holiday tourists and native New Yorkers, all busy in their own individual endeavors. Nope. No one was coming in, but she turned off her open sign. Despite knowing what treasures Giuseppe's Toy Emporium might have to offer any would-be customer, Florida simply couldn't blame anyone for not coming inside. It was much too easy to stay home and browse the internet, and shop online. It was an investment of time for anyone to come inside, and everyone was much too busy and stressed with day to day life to make that investment. It was sad. The magic of the brick and mortar toy store was a relic from another time, and Giusppe's Toy Emporium had gone the way of the dinosaur. Though she was going out of business, she agreed with her father in principle and refused to focus her business online. She did have a website, and a little traffic, it only constituted a very small percentage of her business philosophy. She believed kids need to touch a toy, experience a toy in person before they take it home.

"No, I'm sorry mam, we don't have anything like that in our inventory," a baffled Autumn Giuseppe answered as she listened patiently. She grimaced at her mom. The caller made little sense. "I'm sorry mam, to be honest, I'm a little confused. You say, you saw *this* toy store in a television commercial?" There was more silence as Florida shook her head, "No mam, there must be some sort of mistake, Giuseppe's Toy Emporium isn't running any advertisements on TV at this time."

Florida watched her daughter. *"What an odd phone call..."* she thought to herself.

"Mom, this lady swears she saw a commercial, and our store was featured in it...we're not running any TV ads right now? Are we?"

Florida laughed.

"No. I didn't think we did," Autumn said as she shook her head. "But, I'm telling you, you should have taken this call, this lady *swears...it was our store.*"

"Autumn, what kind of toy did she see in the commercial, maybe we have one or two in stock we can sell her?"

"That's the really weird part mom...I've never heard of this toy before. She called it an Imaginarium Wand."

"The what?" Florida asked, now she was puzzled too. She grew up in the toy business and she'd never heard of anything like that. She shrugged it off, maybe it was an electronic game, or something along those lines, but what an odd name for a toy just the same. It sounded like the name of a toy her father might have drawn up in design, but never built.

She laughed. Nope. Not possible, come to think of it, her father did design a toy he called, "The Imaginarium Wand," but could never get it to work, so he gave the preliminary sketches to Santa Claus during one of his visits to her father's shop. Florida had never met Santa, much less catch a glimpse of him, but her father would talk freely about their visits. It had been years since her family heard from Santa Claus. He stopped coming around after her father passed away.

"An Imaginarium Wand? Hmmm, go figure, someone must've gotten it to work, but I don't see how, it really requires an imaginative play, and unless a toy has a computer chip, or an LED screen, I don't see kids playing with it anymore," Florida thought, *"but, it's our fault as an industry, we were busy chasing dollars, instead of really thinking of kids, and their need to exercise those imaginations."*

"Thank you for calling today, and good luck finding that," Autumn said as she hung up the phone, but before she could take a step away from the phone, it rang again.

Florida looked at the ringing phone in confusion.

"What's going on mom? What should we do, do you think there's been some kind of misadvertisement, and listed our phone number by accident?"

"It's unlikely Autumn. It is odd someone's calling the store, especially twice, but no matter, let it go to voicemail for now. Let's finish closing up, and get some dinner, how's that sound?"

"I'm hungry," Autumn said as she hugged her mom tight. Her mom needed a hug right now. She knew it would really add insult to her mom's situation if a large international *"toy"* company succeeded at making the Imaginarium, and somehow stole her grandfather's idea.

The two got their coats, and hats on, and watched the snow fall through the store's front window. Despite Florida's dreary outlook and mood, she still managed to decorate the front window display for the season. She spent the better part of two days dressing up the store window. Florida spent a considerable amount of time, selecting the toys for the window, laying out the toy trains, and hanging Christmas lights, but despite the grandeur of the window, she knew it would do little to draw in customers inside. It would have been a better use of her time, dressing up their store's webpage, but it was her father's tradition, and it would be their last Christmas.

The phone rang again as Florida opened the store's front door and stepped out into the crisp night air.

"It's ringing off the hook," Autumn said.

"Yeah, too bad it's a wrong number."

Florida saw her answering machine was blinking. There were messages already, waiting for her, but they would all have to wait until after Thanksgiving.

"How's pizza?" Florida asked.

"Famous Ray's Pizza over on West 34th street?" Autumn asked.

"No, I was thinking about Ray's Famous Pizza up on East 41th street."

"I'm starving mom, I don't care," Autumn insisted as they walked away from Giuseppe's Toy Emporium, unaware of the growing number of voicemails.

"Snack on some snowflakes for now," Florida said as she caught snowflakes with her tongue and reached for Autumn's hand.

"I guess it'll have to do for now," Autumn grinned playfully at her mom, and for a moment, could put the failing toy store behind them as they strolled together along Central Park. "The park is so peaceful when it snows."

"Yes it is, I'm grateful it's snowing right now," Florida replied as she took her daughter by the hand, *"And, I'm grateful for you..."*

"Mom, do you realize we forgot today was Thanksgiving?"

"Oh no!" Florida stopped still in her tracks. She did forget. She suddenly felt sad again.

"It's okay mom, I'm grateful for you too. I knew you were preoccupied by the store today, and just not in the spirit."

"It's no excuse, scratch Pizza, where can we have turkey at this hour of the evening?"

"I'm grateful for Pizza mom, I want Pizza for my Thanksgiving dinner."

Florida hugged Autumn as tourists and local New Yorkers walked on by.

"Okay, we're having original New York Pizza for our Thanksgiving." Florida agreed, and took Autumn by the hand again, and the two went off to find the best Pizza in town.

Lulu Jingle

Sledding was epic today, for Lulu Jingle, as she started down another hill. The frost stung her nose, and cheeks as she sailed down the largest hill inside Santa's Castle. This was her favorite hill to sleigh down, because from the very top she could see over the castle walls and watch the other elves work and stay busy. There was an added sense of urgency right now with the elves, because today was Black Friday and down in the Lower Latitudes, it meant Christmas was in twenty-seven days. There was no time for elves to dilly-dally around. They had to focus, and ensure their quotas were met in time for Christmas Eve. An army of elves marched towards Santa's workshop. From the top of the hill, Lulu could see the familiar Gizmo 3000 on the backs of the elves. From a distance the marching elves appeared to be carrying oversized candy canes on their backs.

The design for the Gizmo 3000, giving an appearance of a candy cane, was done out of an abundance of caution by Santa Claus. Santa felt it was prudent to camouflage the true nature of the Gizmo 3000, hiding its wondrous intention from potential foreign operatives, just in case a Gizmo unit fell into the hands of bad actors. If for some reason a spy satellite passed over Santa's Workshop, the Castle, and Elf City, it would only appear the elves were parading around with oversized candy canes.

The day shift elves sang jolly Christmas Carols as they marched into the factory to relieve the night shift. Each elf carried their assigned Gizmo 3000 proudly on their back as they prepared to take it up another notch in the day's quota of toys.

Despite her classroom certificate for the Gizmo 3000, she could never pass field testing to receive a certification on the 3000, because she simply worked too fast for the Gizmo 3000. There were shreds of the Gizmo 3000 piled up, waiting to be melted down, and refurbished into snow plows and snow shovels.

Whenever Lulu Jingle powered on a Gizmo 3000, they would overheat, and blow up into a cloud of tinsel. The 3000 could not contain her Christmas Cheer and Merriment and at the core of every Gizmo, is the heart of an elf. It's our Christmas Cheer and Merriment that powers the Gizmo. Like I said in the beginning of this story, all elves possess the Christmas Spirit, it's just some elves exist on a higher spectrum than the rest of us, and Lulu Jingle is out in the Stratosphere with her Christmas Spirit. In all fairness, she can't help it. Lulu *loves* Christmas, and wants to make toys so badly, and do her part to bring happiness to others, but it takes over her ability to manage a Gizmo model.

All the instructors were forced to hold her back from advancing with the rest of her class, because she was a liability to the production line. If you could see one of those Gizmo 3000s just burn out into tinsel, it's sobering to watch.

Lulu was sent to learn the bakery, but she was all thumbs, and not a good match for the bakery division. She couldn't keep time good enough to be in one of our bands, nor carry a tune, so a career as a full time Christmas Caroler was not very likely. It didn't really matter to Lulu, she wanted to be a toy maker. She knew it was her calling, and she would just have to learn how to dim her Christmas Spirit, but that only made her sad, and a sad elf is almost as bad as an exploding Gizmo Toy Maker.

It seemed Lulu would be forced to ride the hills on a sleigh for a long time, if Santa couldn't help her.

Lulu did her best to not feel discouraged, but it was hard. Each year, she would try out on the Gizmo 3000, only to have it explode into a large ball of tinsel, creating quite a mess. She loved the excitement of Christmas in the Lower Latitudes, and what it meant to millions of people. She wanted to be a part of the joy people felt during the season, and make toys that would make the good boys and girls happy.

Lulu had twinkling blue eyes, a mischievous, but playful grin. She was always willing to help her neighbor, and good friends to many of the woodland animals.

Lulu started on her fourth run down Marshmallow Mountain. Marshmallow Mountain was just within sight of Santa's office window, and he enjoyed watching Lulu from time to time, and likewise, Lulu would often glance up at his office window, hoping one day, he would need her help, somewhere.

On the day Santa called for her, the sledding was exceptional and it seemed the sleigh just flew on the wind as she sped past her Woodland friends.

"Careful Lulu! You don't want another accident at the bottom of Marshmallow Mountain again!" Mother Rabbit yelled as Lulu's sled flew past her, and her young liter of little Rabbits.

"Momma! We want to ride on Lulu's sled, please!" Mother Rabbit's little ones shouted in one voice as they watched Lulu zip effortlessly down towards the bottom of the mountain.

"Absolutely not children!" Mother Rabbit said firmly.

"Aww darn," a more vocal rabbit complained.

"Darwin, that'll be enough, or I'll send you back to the Burrough, and you won't get a glimpse of Santa today."

"I want to see Santa momma, do you think we'll see him today? Darwin asked.

"If Santa is in his office today we will, because Santa always sticks his head out of his office window and waves 'hello' to Lulu Jingle."

"I see a light in the window momma," mentioned another little rabbit.

"Yes Willow, it would appear Santa is in his office today, we'll just have to wait and see.

It was a big deal for the Woodland animals to catch a glimpse of Santa Claus, and many of them stood on the edge of the Forest if they sensed he was in his castle.

Lulu Jingle yelled back over her shoulder towards her woodland friends, "Don't worry guys!" but suddenly Lulu plowed into a large snow drift just beneath Santa's window. There was a solid **THUD** as snow slid off the roof and buried Lulu further in the deep snow drift.

"Oh dear!" Cried one of the birds as they landed nervously on top of the snow drift, "Are you okay Lulu?" Lulu managed to poke her gloved hand out of the snow drift. "She's okay guys!" The nervous bird reported to the other Woodland animals as they scurried, and scampered towards Lulu.

Lulu Jingle dug herself out from the snow. She was laughing as she brushed herself off. As she put her elf hat back on, she noticed her Magic Christmas Bulb was missing from her hat. Lulu dove back into the snow, frantically digging for her personal treasure.

"What's wrong Lulu?" Momma Rabbit asked as she came hopping down towards Lulu with her little ones close behind.

"I believe she's lost her Magic Christmas Bulb," the birds all said in chorus together.

"Oh stop birds, not everything is a song," Momma Rabbit said as she hopped on top of the snow pile, eager to help her friend.

"The birds are right Mother Rabbit, I can't find my Magic Christmas Bulb!"

"Oh dear, I'm certain it's nearby Lulu," Sir Alfred Moose said as he used his large set of antlers to scope snow.

"Oh hello, Sir Alfred Moose, I didn't hear you walk up, but I appreciate your help, you can help me dig for it!" Lulu said as she shook snow from one of her boots.

"Glad to help Lulu, we all saw you take a tumble at the bottom of Marshmallow Mountain and wanted to come to your aid," the large Moose said as he scooped more snow with his antlers.

Lulu's signature, her personal sparkle, and bling were not complete without her Magic Christmas Bulb. Lulu believed her red ornament was where she got her super-elf toy making abilities from. Santa gave her the ornament many years ago, because she was not just high on the Merriment Spectrum, but so high, she caused all of the Gizmo 3000s to simply burst into a ball of tinsel dust. Santa said the Magic Christmas Bulb was a promise to her, a promise that one day, Santa would find her a unique job among his toy makers. She was the only elf in the North Pole with a magic Christmas Bulb, and right now it was buried in this snow bank, possibly...*broken.*

"Lulu Jingle, how is the sleigh riding today?" A familiar, and jolly voice yelled from above.

"Santa!" Lulu yelped, startled by the unexpected surprise! "Eh, I can't find my Magic Christmas Bulb Santa!" Lulu called back up, "I had a particularly nasty run in with this snow bank and I seem to have lost my sparkle."

"Nonsense Lulu Jingle, you always sparkle, even if you've merely temporarily misplaced your Christmas Bulb. I think I see it dangling from Sir Alfred's antlers.

"Hello Santa," the enormous animal called out above to a very jolly Santa Claus.

Lulu glanced up and was thrilled to see her red Magic Christmas Bulb dangling from one of the moose's horns. They were all relieved Lulu's Magic Bulb was once more, safely in her possession.

As Lulu fastened her Magic Christmas Bulb to her hat, Santa called down to her again, "Lulu, are you busy right now, do you think I can pull you away from the sleighing?"

Lulu Jingle froze.

"What would Santa want with me?"

"I'm sure Lulu will be right up!" Mother Rabbit called up to Santa as she nudged her friend to respond.

"Yes Santa! I'll be right there!" Lulu said as she trudged free of the deep snow bank, with the help of her friend the Moose.

"That's good news, because Santa Claus needs Lulu Jingle's help today!"

All of the Woodland animals cheered and whistled for their friend. This was good news! It was *the* break Lulu had been longing for, but whatever would Santa want with the industrious Lulu Jingle? She broke all of the Gizmo 3000s, and there wasn't another job in the North Pole for Lulu Jingle, she was a toy maker at heart, and didn't want to settle for anything less than making toys.

In a dash, Lulu was running towards the entrance to Santa's Castle. Santa waved to the Woodland creatures below.

"Good Morning Mother Rabbit, how's the family this morning?" Santa asked.

"We're doing great Santa," one of the little rabbits replied.

"Santa, my family is doing well, and thank you for asking. We're all so eager for Christmas around our burrow, but can we ask, and I think I speak for all of the Woodland animals when I ask, whatever is going on with Lulu Jingle, should we be concerned for her?"

"Ho! Ho!" Santa laughed, "Not at all my friends, why I have a very important mission for her tonight! It's such an important mission, only Lulu Jingle can accomplish it."

"Oh that sounds important, and very exciting!" Sir Alfred Moose shouted up to Santa.

"I wonder what Santa would need our Lulu Jingle for?" Mother Rabbit whispered to the Moose.

"Lulu Jingle left her sled in the snow," one of the little rabbits pointed to her Mother Rabbit.

"Yes I know Twitchy-Elizabeth, but right now, Lulu Jingle is on a mission for Santa!" Mother Rabbit replied and smiled at her little one.

Lulu was eagerly racing towards the front gate to Santa's Castle. There was no time to remember her trusty sleigh, it would be safe for now under the care of her Woodland friends.

"What does Santa want with Lulu?" another small rabbit asked of his mother.

"I guess we'll have to wait and see, but for now let's head back to the burrow for now."

Lulu passed the Candy Cane Orchard, and Gumdrop trees. She passed the marching Nutcracker soldiers on brightly festive streets. The Nutcrackers marched two across, and one hundred Nutcracker Soldiers long. It was always decorated for Christmas around the North Pole, but extra effort was placed into decorating during *the Christmas season rush.*

"Where are you in such a hurry too?" One of the snowmen yelled after Lulu as she narrowly avoided running into him as she dashed through the center square inside of Santa's grand castle. '

She stopped to apologize, "I'm so sorry Eddie, but Santa called for me!"

Eddie took a moment to fix his hat, and smiled joyful smile, happy for Lulu Jingle and said, "I'm very happy for you Lulu, you've waited a long time for a call from Santa Claus, please let everyone know as soon as you can, what Santa has planned for you!"

"I will Eddie!" Lulu said and waved goodbye to the snowman.

With shiny brass horns, and thumping drums, smartly dressed elves marched through the street and played the elves favorite Christmas Carols. Shopkeepers waved from their front doors as Lulu raced past their storefronts in a pink blur of motion. Lulu had no time to wave back. The street smelled of warm chocolate, cheese, and other delicious Christmas confections. The falling snow smelled fresh as it fell on her nose and burned her cheeks. Lulu darted towards the drawbridge, and over the moat full of sparkling Christmas Cheer. The river was running high, because the tide was high for Christmas, and though the air temperature was below freezing, the Spirit of Christmas kept the water a warm Seventy-Eight Degrees Fahrenheit.

The drawbridge to both Santa's Castle, and Great Hall were never closed. Lulu raced towards the grand staircase that led up to what is known as The Great Hall. The Great Hall is Santa's personal dwelling. She passed napping Polar Bears and caroling Penguins as fast as her little pink boots would carry her as she took two steps at a time. Inside of The Great Hall was Santa's personal workshop, and office. There were so many unknown secrets locked away inside of the Great Hall of Santa Claus.

The Great Hall of Santa Claus

The Great Hall of Santa Claus was as old as time itself. Most things in the North Pole are magical, and the Great Hall is no different. On most days the Great Hall of Santa Claus was built from gold, and polished stone, but occasionally the majestic Hall of Santa Claus might take on an appearance of a whimsical Gingerbread House. Whatever form the Great Hall of Santa Claus took on, it really depended on the mood of the Great Hall. The Great Hall of Santa Claus stood within Santa's Castle, overlooking the Great Woodlands surrounding the hall. In addition to the Great Woodlands, there were mountains, and hills, and many, many friendly animals.

Santa's Castle, and workshop, were just on the outskirts of Elf City. Hidden far away up in the North Pole, and far away from the Lower Latitudes, Elf City was a thriving metropolis. Our way of life, city, Santa's Castle and the Great Hall, were all hidden from foreign governments, and greedy men. No one seemed to know the origins of Santa. There were a few who believed Santa was actually Father Time's brother, a giant kid at heart, and able to live outside of mortal time. It didn't matter where Santa came from, because time never affected Santa like the mortals living in the Lower Latitudes. There were also a few theories floating around that maybe Santa was a time traveler. A time traveler who stopped in for a visit one day, and decided to stick around after he realized he liked building toys.

The Great Hall of Santa Claus was enormous and there wasn't anything like it in the Lower Latitudes. In some circles, the Great Hall is the 8th Wonder of the World, perhaps more wondrous than the Egyptian Pyramids, or the Great Wall of China.

The Great Hall of Santa Claus, sometimes took on different shapes, and sizes. Though the Great Hall was mystical, it was always full of the Christmas Spirit. It was from within the Great Hall, Santa's personal workshop hummed with ideas for new toys, or improvements for the Gizmo 3000. Santa was always perfecting his Gizmo so we could turn out toys faster, and more efficiently. Eventually the Gizmo 4000 was dreamed up, and built to spec, but sadly no elf could safely operate the Gizmo 4000.

There's an observatory on top of the hall, and from his observatory Santa keeps a large telescope pointed towards the night sky and Milky Way. Santa is keen on watching the stars from his home at the North Pole, and perhaps why some believe he is an intergalactic traveler. Some have even speculated Santa feels homesick sometimes for his home among the stars, but if he were, he would never share that with his elves.

If anyone asked him, he would merely say, "Ho! Ho!" and change the subject...

The observatory is manned by a team of elf astronomers, yes, there are astronomers in the North Pole, and a complete "North Pole U" but not to be convinced with the *U of Miami.*

At the U of the North Pole, the brightest elves pull their minds together to learn the sciences and study literature from around the world. They catalog history, writing it down in volumes to store in the Great Library inside of the University. They advance the cause of elves, and pass on what they learn to Santa so he can use that research to help better the lives of men and women in the Lower Latitudes. Santa believes in the pursuit of knowledge and learning, and any elf that expresses a desire to go to the *U,* Santa accommodates that pursuit. Santa is so keen on knowledge, and education, he even set up a Dentistry School at the University after one elf expressed a need.

Within the North Pole City there exists both an airport, and heliport, because two weeks out of the year, elves will travel to somewhere in the Lower Latitudes for vacation, usually somewhere warm. Phoenix, Arubia, and Palm Springs are the preferred destinations, followed by Oahu. There's only one airplane, so the elves have to book their vacations in advance. The helicopter is great for getting around the city in a hurry, and keeping up with the traffic and Caribou herd reports.

There's also a standing army of Nutcrackers. Brightly arrayed, smartly uniformed, the armies parade in the streets, and stand watch on the castle walls surrounding the city and Santa's Castle. The Nutcracker army never gets tired, never gets cold, and remains steadfast in the protection of the city.

There's rail service around the city, and to distant places in the far reaches of the North Pole, because from these remote places, the Northern Lights feel close enough to touch. There's clans of elves who choose to live outside of the city, preferring the quiet of the isolation. They live among themselves, and commute into the city on a single rickety trolley and equally rickety track. For some elves, the city can feel too lively, and merrymaking seven days a week can take a toll so it's nice to ride the rickety trolley back to the quiet hamlets outside of the city, and get away from it all.

However, Lulu Jingle was not one of those elves who preferred solitude and preferred to live in the center of the city. Lulu's loft apartment had a good view of the Great Hall, and depending on what shape the hall grew into that morning, Lulu could catch an occasional glimpse of Santa's office window. On many nights Lulu Jingle, doused the candle in her apartment, and sat in the dark, watching Santa's office window, hoping the call would come.

"When can I help?" She often wondered out loud to herself, careful to not get grumpy, because she was careful to not wither, or dither away her Christmas Spirit.

Lulu wanted to build toys, but her spirit was too much for the Gizmo, so unless Santa reconfigured a Gizmo for Lulu, she would just have to remain patient, and remain on the sidelines.

As Lulu climbed the Grand Staircase inside of the Great Hall she was a radiant beam of joy, grinning from ear to ear. The stairs twisted, spiraling up, and up, as Lulu ran two stairs at a time as she raced in breathless anticipation.

"Wherever are you running too?" General McElf asked as she ran past the infamous commander of the Nutcracker Army.

Like any head of state, Santa Claus needed security too, and General McElf was the head of Santa's security and army. Whenever Santa traveled in the Lower Latitudes without his sleigh and Eight Tiny Reindeer a detachment of Nutcrackers remained on alert, just in case there was trouble, but fortunately, they've never been called on for help.

"Santa Claus wants me to come see him, General McElf!"

"Well slow yourself Lulu before you cause an accident on the stairs today, they have a mind of their own, and they're acting a bit mischievous today!" the grumpy general warned.

"I will General, I'm terribly sorry!"

"These stairs are an enigma, and can confound even the wisest elf" the General muttered under his breath as he paused to fix his large fur hat, and smooth over his many ribbons and medals, before once more descending down the long, spiral staircase. The distinguished general smiled beneath his white beard. He was happy to see Lulu running towards her own destiny. Santa filled the general in on Lulu's mission, just in case Lulu's mission were compromised, and she needed a rescue mission back to the North Pole. She was a good kid, he thought to himself, and if any elf had a chance for mission success, especially this important mission, it was Lulu Jingle.

Lulu raced past singing toys and pokey reindeer.

"Excuse me Donner, Prancer, and Vixen!" Lulu gleefully shouted as she eagerly pushed past the reindeer, creating quite a commotion.

"Sorry we're moving a little slow today Lulu, we're all a little sore from our reindeer games," Prancer said apologetically.

"No worries, but you should really get some rest guys! Christmas is in Twenty-Seven Days!"

Lulu ran higher, and higher on the grand, twisting staircase, so far, and so high, Lulu started feeling as if she were going to soon run among the clouds. The Grand Staircase inside of the hall was a fickle one. It was enchanted, and like the rest of the Great Hall of Santa Claus, the Grand Staircase was simply magical. The staircase never felt the same, and on some days, the staircase seemed longer than the day before. Some days the stairs had landings that weren't there the day before, and on other days, the staircase felt shorter than on other days. Some days the stairs were cobbled by wood, and on other days, they were made from polished granite. On occasion, the staircase was fashioned from diamond.

Like everything in the North Pole, no one from the Lower Latitudes could find the City of Elves, or Santa's Castle. Even though the North Pole was mapped out by explorers from the Lower Latitudes, and observed from space by the International Space Station, and by various spy satellites, we remained hidden by magic.

It was said, when you came to the first step of the Grand Staircase, only those with the Christmas Spirit would ever find their way off the stairs, because if you doubted Christmas, the stairs would just go on forever. One landing, to another landing, one more stair, followed by another stair, up, or down, it wouldn't matter, the Grand Staircase was a test of your Christmas Spirit, and if you lacked spirit, the staircase would hold you on its stairs, and never let you off. They were also meant to protect Santa's most guarded secrets, because anyone wanting to steal those secrets from Santa's office, would have to first climb the Grand Staircase, and reveal their nature to those enchanted stairs.

Finally after what seemed like hours of endless climbing, Lulu Jingle got to the top of the Grand Staircase, and peered out a hall of windows. From the hall of windows, Lulu Jingle could see what looked like a kingdom below. A Christmas Kingdom of sorts she thought to herself. From a distance Elf City glowed with Christmas Cheer, and buzzed with industrious motion, and commotion. From far below, the sounds of Christmas Carols drifted cheerfully up to her pointed ears. Lulu couldn't help but twirl, and dance as she listened to the joy below. It was finally Christmas, and Santa was waiting to see her!

"Oh my, how could I forget! I can't dither, and keep Santa waiting!" Lulu snapped back to her purpose at hand.

She knocked on a heavy, decorative wooden door. An office door fitting for Santa Claus.

"Ho! Ho! Is that Lulu Jingle outside of my door?" A cheerful, familiar voice called from behind the heavy oak door.

Lulu snapped to attention, and saluted the closed door.

"Yes Sir! Lulu Jingle reporting for duty Santa!"

"Come on in Lulu, time is short, and we need to get started immediately," Santa replied as Lulu pulled the heavy door wide open. Lulu was dwarfed by the enormous doorway as she stepped inside nervously.

"Step inside Lulu, I will need your help in New York City tonight!" Santa Claus said as he jumped up from behind his large desk.

Lulu was stunned.

"New York City Santa?"

Lulu knew this was the place to be. All over the world during the Christmas Season, children sat on a costumed actor's lap, an actor pretending to be Santa Claus for the benefit of children. The children would tell the Santa Claus actor what they wanted for Christmas, and the actor would play the role, some better than others, and the whole moment was done in shopping malls, and community centers throughout the Lower Latitudes, but Lulu Jingle was actually standing in Santa Claus' own place of solitude, his office, his personal space to create. *This was Santa's office!* Lulu knew many pretend-Santa's and their corporate handlers tried to create Santa's world for the benefit of the children, but many got it wrong. Santa's desk was cluttered with blue prints, and a coffee mug. Santa drank coffee when he was home in the office, not hot chocolate, or milk. Many mall Santas sat on fancy, decorative chairs, but the *actual* Santa sat on a regular, squeaky office chair, with a seat cushion, and lumbar support. Santa was not given to tidy workspaces. His desk was cluttered with rolls of paper, a small typewriter, because Santa often typed daily to-do lists, or an occasional memo. In fact, Lulu counted four coffee mugs scattered around his office, because Santa was so fond of coffee throughout the day as he worked. Santa refused to bring on a personal office assistant or secretary, and for a moment, Lulu was worried perhaps he was considering asking Lulu to help him around his cluttered office. Santa also refused to use his magic, because he felt old fashioned work effort is what kept him spry, not magic.

Lulu Jingle stood at attention, because she was ready to serve her commander and chief!

Santa laughed a deep, jolly laugh as he contemplated Lulu.

Lulu smiled. She understood why Santa Claus was so loved by millions. He radiated joy, and love for others.

Santa continued to laugh as he took his reading glasses off.

"You've been very patient Lulu Jingle," he said to her.

"Yes Santa, but I'm ready to do my part..." she replied, but still unsure what Santa might want with her today. She simply could not work the Gizmo 3000, and her heart was determined to build toys.

"You weren't hurt this morning, were you?"

"Santa?"

"Why at the bottom of Marshmallow Mountain, just below my office window this morning," Santa answered. "I need you in tip-top shape, Lulu Jingle."

Lulu could only shake her head. She was so grateful she wasn't hurt this morning, because that would have been a terrible break for her. It would have been a very sad affair, if she'd been hurt on the very morning Santa asked for help from her. Getting a call from Santa Claus was like getting called up from the minor leagues to the major leagues! As the clouds drifted by Santa's office window, Lulu tried to not get distracted, because just a few minutes ago, Santa's office window appeared a few feet above her, and she had run up many flights of stairs to get to his office, but the elves in the North Pole have learned to just go with the flow. Lulu cleared her head. She couldn't let her excitement distract her from the conversation at hand with Santa Claus.

"Nope, not a scratch Santa. I only lost my Magic Christmas ball for a moment, but Moose helped me find it! Do you remember when you gave me this Magic Christmas Ornament? You told me it came off your personal Christmas Tree." What a silly question to ask of Santa Claus, of course he remembered giving her an ornament of his personal Christmas tree.

Santa chuckled, "Ho, Ho Lulu Jingle, of course I remember your magic Christmas Ball. It came from my personal Christmas tree. Santa pointed to a large glowing Christmas tree on the other side of his office.

Lulu gasped when she saw the Christmas Tree. From what she'd heard from the other elves, this was the original, very first Christmas tree. Legend has it, *this* Christmas tree was the source of all the magic around the North Pole. It was the eternal Christmas Tree. This Christmas Tree never withered, and though it was planted in Santa's Castle, it never faded and dried. Its needles were forever green, and the festive lights and decorative decorations twinkled as bright as the stars. This was the inspiration for all Christmas trees!

It was from this very tree her special ornament came from. It was taken from a branch by Santa Claus, and given to her as a promise.

"All elves have purpose Lulu Jingle, and I promise one day your purpose will be revealed, but for now, we have to be patient, until that time comes whenever you question this, I want you to remember this Christmas Bulb from my own tree. It's my promise to you Lulu."

Though her heart had been broken each time a Gizmo 3000 went POOF and turned into a shiny cloud of tinsel dust, and she had become a liability on the production line, Lulu believed in Santa's promise to her. Lulu sewed her Christmas ornament to her hat so the other elves could see Santa's promise to her.

"I always knew you had such a unique gift, and with a unique gift, you would require a unique purpose. You're a spitfire, a tornado of Christmas cheer, and a passionate toy maker, but until now, the Gizmo 3000 could never hope to match your Christmas Spirit, but that was yesterday, and this is today!"

Lulu just stood in silence. She was in a daze. She wanted to pinch herself, just to make sure she wasn't dreaming any of this!

"It took some time Lulu, but you can't rush purpose. Everything has a time, and a season, and in due time, we'd discover yours, and today I'm going to share with you what your role will be during this Christmas season, and most likely, going forward, because I suspect, there'll be a great demand for this new toy."

"Wow" was the only reaction Lulu could muster at the moment.

"Ho! Ho!" Her commander in chief laughed as he poured himself another cup of coffee and sipped on it. "Ahh that's good," he said as he smiled and smelled the aroma of fresh coffee, "I'll be honest, I get so tired of hot chocolate and milk by the end of the season, but I never tire of my coffee Lulu."

Lulu remained speechless, her moment was finally here!

"Time is short Lulu, so I'll just get to the point, are you familiar with the Gizmo 4000?"

"Yes sir I am," she replied. She was also aware there were issues with the 4000. None of the elves could handle the Gizmo 4000 without it blowing up into a cloud of tinsel. Tinsel was messy stuff, and very hard to clean up, and when a 4000 blew up, it could take days to clean up. One Gizmo 4000 equaled 1000 elves working at full speed, but no elf under the sun could hope to harness the power of its Christmas Spirit.

"To be honest Lulu, I'm a little embarrassed that I haven't thought of this sooner, but like I say, you can't rush purpose, and all things that are good have a way of revealing themselves at the appointed time. None of the elves could handle the Gizmo 4000 safely, because time and again, the 4000 would blow up in a cloud of tinsel dust. Tinsel was messy stuff and the clean up for a blown Gizmo took the effort of many elves from over at the North Pole Public Works Department. Whereas one Gizmo 3000 equaled three thousand human toymaker hours, a Gizmo 4000 equaled four thousand hours, but the four thousand hours was a quantum leap in energy expenditure for any elf to try and manage. It just couldn't be handled, safely.

"Lulu, I will just get to the point, because there's not much time. I have a friend in trouble. A friend in New York City. A friend I owe a debt of gratitude too, and I believe you're the elf to help my friend's ailing toy store." *Lulu was silent.* She wanted to pinch her small pointed ears, rub her rosy red, pointed nose and jump up and down, just to prove to herself she wasn't imagining this conversation. Maybe she'd hit her head at the bottom of Marshmallow Mountain? Maybe she was still lying at the bottom of the hill, dreaming all of this. Nope, she smelled Santa's freshly brewed pot of coffee. He was asking for help!

"It would be a personal favor to me. There's a toy store, a forgotten toy store, and if we don't help my friend, this will be their last Christmas."

"Oh dear," Lulu whispered. The loss of a toy store was indeed something very sad to Santa, and the elves.

"I believe you can help Lulu. I believe you're the only Elf who can use the Gizmo 4000 to craft such a unique toy. Not only will I need you to build a unique toy, I will need you to build enough of those toys to meet a big demand. A very big demand, because as we speak, the wheels are set in motion to build this demand. A toy that at the moment, only exists in sketches."

"The Gizmo 4000 Santa?" Lulu gasped.

"Yes Lulu, I believe I can see your purpose today. Clear as a bell. It's your destiny Lulu! I believe the Gizmo 4000 was made, just for you." Lulu's head was spinning. She'd heard of the Gizmo 4000, but she'd never actually seen the 4000. Lulu was known to break the Gizmo 3000, because her Christmas Spirit was just too much for the 3000. Whenever Lulu picked up the Gizmo 3000, and powered one on, it would just make a loud WHIRL, CLUNK, and POOF followed by one very large cloud of tinsel dust. The tinsel dust would cover all the elves for one quarter mile. It was always quite a mess for The North Pole Public Works Department to try and gather up.

Lulu Jingle was suddenly aware of the doubt creeping into her heart, and if this doubt were left unchecked, it could squelch some of her Christmas Spirit. She didn't have any experience building toys, and now Santa Claus was asking her to rescue a toy store. It wasn't *just* any toy store, it was a toy store that belongs to a friend of Santas. Lulu was starting to feel sad, because she knew she was doubting herself. Doubt was like a weed in a garden full of hopeful flowers. Lulu Jingle couldn't forget her track record with the Gizmo 3000. There were piles of tinsel dust in the scrap yard, because she'd blown so many Gizmos.

"Santa sir, I appreciate your kindness, but I just don't see how it's possible," as she looked down at her pointy boots.

"Nonsense Lulu Jingle, this moment was meant for you. This is your destiny, your purpose, because only you can harness the power of the Gizmo 4000."

"...but Santa, it's never *actually* gone past trials," Lulu reminded him, but she was careful to not actually sound like she was second guessing Santa Claus.

Santa was patient with Lulu. He was wise, and compassionate, and he knew the small elf only needed reassurance. She was a cauldron of Christmas energy, a tempest of Christmas Spirit and a whirlwind of chaotic joyful energy, and perfect for this mission. Lulu Jingle was the only elf who could safely operate the Gizmo 4000, and the Gizmo 4000 was the only instrument on hand he could rely on to help Giuseppe's Toy Emporium.

"Time is short Lulu. I trust you."

"Yes sir!" Lulu snapped as she saluted her Commander and Chief.

"This is important, Lulu. This toy can rescue my friend's toy store. Not only will this toy rescue my friend's toy store, but I believe it will help return the joy of imagination."

"I understand Santa," she said. Santa needed her. There was a toy store in trouble somewhere, and Santa was sending her in! She would have to master the Gizmo 4000 while on the job. It was more powerful than an untamed bucking bronco. More brilliant than a jagged arc of lightning on a stormy dark night, but pound for pound, the Gizmo 4000 would soon meet its match in Lulu Jingle. Lulu had experienced some sadness and disappointment, but she never stopped believing in herself and one day, Santa would have a place for her in the North Pole.

"The Imaginarium Wand!" Santa said abruptly.

He went over to an old painted portrait of himself. Lulu strangely, just noticed the painting on the wall, though she was certain there was nothing hanging on that very wall a few minutes ago. Elves learned to just go with the flow whenever they were inside of Santa's Castle, and the Great Hall.

Santa removed the portrait of himself and spun the dial to his wall safe, waited a moment and pulled open the heavy door. From within the safe, he removed an old dusty looking sketch.

"Come over Lulu and have a look!"

Lulu stepped cautiously towards Santa's desk and looked at his sacred concept drawings scattered everywhere. This was an honor, very few elves ever had the chance to see Santa's raw concept drawings. "My plan is to see the Imaginarium Wand in every home in the Lower Latitudes. Lulu, this is revolutionary, and my hope is the Imaginarium Wand will help restore children's desire to use their imagination while they play!"

Lulu felt excited to be a part of this. She beamed with joy as she looked at the whimsical, sparkling toy on paper.

"This is exciting Santa, but what is the Imaginarium Wand? I don't think I've ever seen any toy like this before."

"That's correct Lulu, because there's never been a toy like this. It's more than a toy, it's a wand of potential, unlimited access to whatever the mind can conceive within any child's imagination to play. Lulu, it's been my experience, sometimes children were most happy playing with a large cardboard box. A cardboard box could offer up the potential to become a fort, a boat, perhaps a racecar. Sandboxes, slides, and even a discarded stick were used for imaginative play. These mundane items offered a child hours of play, and an exercise for the imaginative mind."

Lulu seemed to understand where Santa was going with this.

"That's right Lulu Jingle, the Imaginarium Wand works on this premise, but it's so much better than those discarded items, because the Imaginarium Wand has the look and feel of a shiny, new toy a child might see in a toy store window!"

"Oh Santa, that's so exciting, I can remember the joy children felt when they visited toy stores, or saw the decorations in the store front windows in their towns, and cities!"

Santa grinned and stirred his coffee, "*It needs more sugar...*" he muttered under his breath, as he walked over to a hutch on a wall. Lulu just noticed the shelf, and couldn't remember if a shelf was there just a moment ago. Santa poured a generous amount of sugar in his Santa Claus shaped coffee mug.

"Santa?" Lulu blurted out quizzically. Hesitating, because she understood Santa Claus was relying on her bolt of energy and the powerful Christmas ornament, and any doubt she might have, risked losing some of her Christmas Joy.

"Speak freely Lulu, don't be afraid to ask questions." Santa took another sip of coffee and smiled with contentment, "that's so good."

Lulu grinned, she'd never known Santa was such a big coffee drinker, she just assumed he liked Hot Chocolate, Eggnog, and Milk.

"Why the Gizmo 4000? Why can't we use the Gizmo 3000 to craft the Imaginarium Wand?"

"Oh how rude of me Lulu, would you like a cup of coffee? I can pour you a cup too," Santa asked.

"No thank you Santa, but I appreciate it sir."

"Nonsense, no formalities here Lulu Jingle, but back to your question my little whirlwind of Christmas Spirit. My belief is the Imaginarium will be the hot toy of this Christmas season, and every child in the Lower Latitudes will want one under their tree this Christmas!"

"Every child in the Lower Latitudes Santa?" Lulu gulped. *How many Imaginarium Wands would Santa really need...in one night?*

"Yes Lulu, pretty much every child, I suspect there'll be a plus, or minus of demand for them by three percentage points."

"Our usual baked in quota Santa?" Lulu asked.

"Yes Lulu, I believe there'll be such demand for the Imaginarium Wand, we'll need enough for every child, plus a few extra on hand, because I also think there'll be some parents that will likewise want their own Imaginarium Wand."

"I understand Santa," Lulu asked as she stood at attention.

"Ho! Ho! Make no mistake Lulu Jingle, you are the elf for this mission, and *only* the Gizmo 4000 is powerful enough to craft enough of those Imaginarium Wands!"

Lulu nodded. She would do this! She was the elf for this, and though she was nervous, Lulu knew what it took to power up a Gizmo 3000, but armed with a Gizmo 4000 toy maker, Lulu felt invisible and she was ready to help Santa. She wanted all the kids to have an Imaginarium Wand under their tree, and help Santa's friend in need.

"Do you have any more questions for me Lulu?"

"Just one more Santa, what is the name of your friend's toy store?"

"Yes of course Lulu. Giuseppe's Toy Emporium in New York City."

"Giuseppe's Toy Emporium?" Lulu asked in disbelief. Giuseppe's Toy

Emporium was legendary in the North Pole. She didn't understand why they were in need of Santa's help.

"I know what you're thinking, Lulu. Salvador Giuseppe passed away a few years ago, and economic times have changed, and people are no longer visiting his store like they used to. Parent's prefer to shop online for their children's toys, or visit large retail stores. Small, independent, family owned toy stores are unable to keep up."

"I want to help Santa, this is very important..."

"Yes, it is Lulu. I'll be very busy up here in the North Pole doing last minute preparations for the upcoming Christmas rush, and I'm not able to personally go down to New York City and build the Imaginarium Wand, so I'm sending one of my top elves to do the job for me."

"Eureka Santa! I understand the plan. I'll build enough of the Imaginarium Wand in one night, and come this Christmas season, parents will come looking for theImaginarium Wand at Giuseppe's Toy Emporium!"

Santa eased into his squeaky, rickety office chair, and sipped more on his coffee. His coffee mug, shaped like Santa, was both chipped, and worn. Everything about Santa's office looked worn, old, and yet it was vibrant and magical. Rich in tradition, and history. Smelling of burning firewood, coffee, leather, and Christmas Cookies.

"Cookie Lulu?"

Lulu smiled, she knew for a fact the plate of Christmas Cookies wasn't there a few minutes ago. She just accepted it!

"No thank you Santa."

"Just came out of the oven by the way. If you change your mind, I'll send a dozen with you, but back on point, because time is slipping, and we don't have much of it. You're right Lulu Jingle, there'll be so much demand, and only one place to purchase this sought after toy, my old friend's legacy will live on now."

The cookies on the plate looked delicious, and Lulu was so excited she forgot she'd miss lunch in the Great Dining Hall. She smiled, and picked up a frosted sugar cookie and nibbled on it. It was delicious, baked directly in Santa's personal oven, wherever that might be.

"Take a dozen with you Lulu. You'll need your strength tonight. Salvador's toy store is a wondrous place, especially back in the glory days of toy stores. During the decades after World War Two, the 50s, and up until the age of the internet, parents went to their local toy store, or shopped from a catalog. Children were enthralled with looking at toys in a catalog, or watching them from a toy store window. It was an experience, sadly gone now from the Lower Latitudes. There's a lot of *rush-rush*, and very little personalized experiences, and little room for memories to be made during Christmas. Today, parents point, click, drop, ship, and in a day, or two, their parcels arrive without much fanfare.

"This is sad Santa. Toys are special, and I consider it an honor to build a toy children will want under their tree."

"Yes Lulu, a child's relationship with a toy is unique, and depending on the toy, it can last for many years, and create many fond memories for them later in life."

"What does the Imaginarium Wand do Santa?" Her eyes were starting to twinkle from anticipation.

"The Imaginarium Wand can create anything, or any moment a child can see, or conjure up with their imagination. I'll let you in on a little secret Lulu, there is a dash of magic in each Imaginarium Wand, I mean, you can't have a wand without magic, but it's nominal, not very much, just enough to create a sparkle and twinkle!"

"Why can't kids just use their imaginations, without the wand sir?"

Santa chuckled. He smiled at the small, quizzical elf.

"All very good questions Lulu, and since you're my chief builder for the Imaginarium Wand, it's very important that you understand this top down!"

Lulu wiped the cookie crumbs onto her pink sleeve and saluted again at her Commander in Chief. Despite his insistence she not be formal, she couldn't help but salute. In fact, all the elves revered the one and only, Saint Nicholas, Father Christmas, and Papai Noel. Santa Claus had many names, but despite his mythical nature, and global footprint during the Christmas season in the Lower Latitudes, he remained humble in nature, and full of Christmas Joy.

"You're absolutely right Lulu. Children do have an imagination, but sadly, many of the toys manufactured today, do the playing for children. A child will turn on a toy today, and the toy presents a one dimensional experience, and once the experience is done, the toy is discarded for something new. The toy creates an experience for the child. Children used to create an experience with their toys. Imaginations were robust, and very active."

"Eureka! When do I leave?" Lulu shouted as she stuffed another Christmas Cookie in her mouth. Lulu felt as if she were a rocket about to blast off. A rocket powered by the spirit of Christmas.

"Tonight Lulu. I'll go over the Imaginarium Wand in detail with you, and also give you a brief tutorial of the Gizmo 4000."

Giuseppe's Toy Emporium

Several people passing Giuseppe's Toy Emporium paused when they thought they heard a crash from the roof above them. After several moments, they shrugged it off and continued on past the darkened toy store. Giuseppe's Toy Emporium was closed for the day. The day before Black Friday. The day after Thanksgiving. It was the day when the mad rush of shopping began for the upcoming Christmas Season. Shopping Mall Santas would get inundated with kids, and parents as they patiently.

Little did anyone know, it was also the day in the North Pole when the elves were in a mad rush to finish preparations for Christmas Eve. Everyone in the Lower Latitudes thought they had an idea what it was like on Black Friday, and the days leading up to Christmas Eve, but in actuality it was much, much more chaotic for the elves. Even in the final minutes leading up to the moment Santa's sleigh left from the North Pole, it was quite an exercise of rushing around. Black Friday wasn't just the kickoff day for parents to shop for their families, it was the *two minute* warning up in the North Pole.

The sound that came from the roof of Giuseppe's Toy Emporium sounded like a hundred metal trash cans, falling down a hundred flight of steps as Lulu Jingle landed on the roof with such a chaotic clatter, but despite the ruckus, and a curious stray cat, none of the New Yorkers knew Lulu Jingle was in the Big Apple. It was late Thanksgiving, and tomorrow morning the shopping would begin, and Lulu had exactly one night to stock the shelves with enough Imaginarium Wands to go around for pretty much every child in the Lower Latitudes. The question as to whether the toy store had enough shelf space for that many wands was irrelevant to Lulu, because like everything else in the North Pole, you just had to accept it, and go with the flow. *Somehow, there would just be enough shelf space to go around to accommodate all of the toys...*

Lulu waved at Santa's sleigh as he flew back to the North Pole. She was alone now, on top of the roof of Giuseppe's Toy Emporium. Just that morning she was sleigh riding on Marshmallow Mountain, and spending the morning with her Woodland friends. She barely had time to rush out to them and tell them the exciting news. They were all very excited for Lulu as they listened to Santa's plan for her, the Gizmo 4000, and the Imaginarium Wand. The Woodland animals were all very heartened to hear the good news about Giuseppe's Toy Emporium.

Lulu made friends everywhere she went. Elves, animals, it didn't matter. Lulu Jingle's joy, and Christmas Spirit were infectious and it enabled her to make friends with the Woodland animals. Very few elves took the time to talk to the animals back home in the North Pole. They were all very busy, or rushing around and much too busy to visit with the Woodland animals in the Great Wood surrounding Elf City, or Santa's Castle. Only Santa took time to make friends in the Great Wood, and knew all of the animals by first name. Sometimes, even the North Pole could feel similar to the Big Apple as Lulu peered over the ledge of Giuseppe's Toy Emporium. She saw the sky scrappers. The taxis, buses and cars drove about as they passed rushing pedestrians. To her, New York City reminded her of Elf City.

A light snow was starting to fall as Lulu felt the weight of the Gizmo 4000 on her back. If anyone caught a glimpse of her, they would just assume a small child was carrying around a very large, oversized candy cane on their back. With a twitch of her nose, Lulu was down the fire escape, and just outside of an upstairs window. It was a good thing, Santa Claus sprinkled a little magic dust over her after she fell out of his sleigh and onto the roof. He sighed, and said she might need just a little help navigating her way around New York, and a little magic dust would go a long way in helping her sort things out during her stay.

"Wow, that was intense!" As she gathered her bearings after twitching her nose and suddenly found herself standing on a fire escape instead of the roof.

The stray cat followed her down the fire escape as she felt the familiar weight of the Gizmo 4000. She could feel a slight hum within its internal processors and various flanges, and out-vents. It crackled and made the fine hair on her arms stand up from its energized core and static charge. In her coat pocket she carried the sketch for the Imaginarium Wand. She twitched her nose again like Santa Claus taught her, and before she could say, "Merry Christmas" the window to Giuseppe's Toy Emporium popped open its lock for her.

"This is a nifty trick," she thought to herself. Lulu wished she had time to play around with the nose twitch thingy, but time was limited. Santa taught her how he uses the nose twitch to access chimneys and windows as he delivers toys on Christmas Eve.

Lulu stepped cautiously inside of the toy store. It was quiet inside, and Lulu Jingle thought to herself, *"Not a creature was stirring."* She giggled at her cleverness, but before she could close the window, a stray cat leaped through the window and insisted on following her inside.

"Oh, hello friend, my name is Lulu Jingle!"

The cat said nothing for a moment, and appeared confused as if something unfamiliar came over it. The stray cat shook off the bedazzled Christmas magic dust, Lulu used to move herself around, and pop open locks. The sparkling dust floated up into the air, and lingered a moment before fading away. Lulu felt inside of her pocket, and removed a small, red velvet bag, she still had plenty of magic dust for the night. She felt confident in her Christmas Cheer, and would do just fine crafting enough Imaginarium Wands, but she really didn't understand how to teleport herself around, or open locked windows without the dust. The cat still remained silent. He appeared a little annoyed, and confused.

"Oh I forgot, we're not in the North Pole right now, and you can't talk. I'll need to use some more of this magic Christmas dust, Santa gave to me, but back home, there's so much magic in the air, the Woodland animals can talk, and Reindeer fly. It's quite amazing my friend!"

Lulu took a pinch of sparkling magic dust from her red velvet bag, and blew it onto the small tabby cat.

"Good. That should fix that, I hope we can be friends! If we are friends, you'd be my very first friend in New York City. Did I tell you, this is my first time here? It looked all very grand from Santa's sleigh as we flew over it, but unfortunately, I won't get to see much of your City tonight, as I have a very important job to do here in this fine establishment."

The cat stood up and stretched before sitting back down to groom his paws some more.

"Hmm. Delayed reaction? You're still a quiet one, maybe you're an introvert, back home in the North Pole, the cats will really talk an elf's ears off. I thought we'd really be chatting it up by now, maybe I didn't use enough of this dust. Here, have more..."

Lulu removed a handful of Magic Christmas Dust and let it sparkle in her hand for a moment.

"It's really beautiful to look at it, isn't it? Do you know the family that owns this toy store? I came here to specifically help them out of a jam. Well, here it goes..."

Lulu threw a handful of the magic dust at the tabby cat. It went POOF and the small cat suddenly coughed, spat, and shook his face abruptly.

"Enough with the dust!" The cat suddenly belted out to Lulu.

The cat coughed out stardust, and snowflakes as it tried to come to terms with its sudden ability to speak to the elf.

"Oh I'm so sorry. I forget my own strength sometimes, but I guess this is why Santa Claus sent me here to craft the Imaginarium Wand with the Gizmo 4000.

"Did I just talk, because I'm very confused by all of this...who are you?"

"Do I detect a French Quebec accent?" Lulu asked.

"Huh? No, New Jersey lady."

"Oh okay, what do I know about Cajun, or Creole accents, this is my first trip to the Lower Latitudes, and I've never heard an accent outside of the North Pole."

"I caught a ride on a ferry sometime ago, and I like it over here in Manhattan, so I decided to stick around," the Cat explained.

"Oh okay, but to answer your question, my name is Lulu Jingle, and I'm here on an important mission from the North Pole."

"Okay, well that makes sense," the cat sarcastically.

"Don't believe me? Well explain why you're talking to me right now."

"Maybe I had some bad fish somewhere, but you have a point, so I'm inclined to believe you a little. Anyways Lulu Jingle, from the North Pole, welcome to New York City. Since this is your first time in New York, let me tell you about the dolts walking around out there, and believe me, I have a lot to say."

"Easy there my feline friend, you just might want to be careful, because you don't want Santa Claus to hear your sour words, and put you on the Naughty List."

The talking cat looked somewhat reluctant for a moment to consider the elf's advice, because he was going to have so much fun with the dogs now. Maybe he would feel less salty with the humans, because of the elf's advice, but the dogs were fair game going forward.

"Hear boy!" the cat thought to himself, and snickered a little at the endless possibility this would offer to him.

"What's your name my friend?" Lulu asked.

"I don't know to be honest," the cat replied, "I've been called a few names, but I've been roaming the streets most of my life. I've never had a family, or person to offer me a name."

"You need a name if we're going to work together. I'm sorry you don't have a family, but I'll be your friend, if you like?"

"I would really like that," the cat said as it started to purr and feel less salty towards the dogs, and humans.

"How about Jingles, because I really like my name, and since we're friends now, it would make sense to me!"

"It has a nice ring to it. Yes, I think I rather like that name. Thank you for your kindness Lulu. I'm sorry if I came across a little sour, I've been feeling a little cross lately. The city has gone to the dogs lately," Jingles said.

"I'm glad we're friends, and now that we're friends, I could use your help tonight!"

"Sure, anything I can do to help a friend, what's your plan while you're in town?"

Lulu pulled the Gizmo 4000 out from a large, red sack, one of Santa's retired toy sacks.

"Wow, that's really interesting Lulu. To be honest, when I first saw you breaking into this store, and that large sack on your back, I really thought you were a cat burglar."

"Burglar?" Lulu asked, "No never!"

"It's a play on words, 'cat' get it?"

"No, I'm sorry," Lulu said confused, "I'm here to craft the Imaginarium Wand tonight."

"It's okay, it's a dumb joke, but back on point, what's the Imaginarium Wand Lulu Jingle, and how can I help you?"

"The Imaginarium Wand will inspire children to create infinite ways to play. They won't be bound by the limitations of a toy that creates the moment for them."

"Ohhh okay," Jingles replied, "Next question, where do I fit in our enterprise?"

"I have to make a lot of wands, and I'm afraid the Gizmo 4000 might draw some unwanted attention, so I need you to keep an eye out for me, perhaps you can sit up in the front window and act as my look out?"

"Sure can!" Jingles said cheerfully as he started to bound towards the front window. "Lulu, I hate to be a bother, because I know you're going to be busy, but what is the Gizmo 4000?"

Lulu wiped the Gizmo 4000 with a lint cloth. She picked up a shoulder harness and buckled herself into the Candy Cane looking instrument.

"This is the Gizmo 4000 Jingles. It harnesses the power of 4000 elves working at once. When you think of the number four thousand, just think, 'Horsepower.'"

"Oh, like an engines Horsepower?"

"Eureka Jingles, that's correct! You're a smart cat! You'll make a fine sentry tonight," Lulu said as she put on a pair of welder's goggles.

"I'll leave you to the mission at hand my fine elf, while I go stand watch!"

Jingles darted to the front window and made himself comfortable in the window display. He was careful to not knock over the many decorative toys and Christmas decorations in the window. As people passed Giuseppe's Toy Store, Jingles was careful to try and go unnoticed by them.

"This shouldn't be too hard," he thought, *"as a stray, they've never noticed me before, I doubt they'll notice me now."*

There was a sudden bright light coming from the back of the store and the strong odor of cinnamon.

"Hey! I think someone might see that light Lulu!" This was exciting. He felt like he had an important purpose right now. Up until now, Jingles never had a friend, and now he was helping an elf build toys. *"Life sure is crazy sometimes..."*

The Gizmo 4000 Powers Up

Lulu gripped the heavy Gizmo 4000 in her gloved hands. It felt sturdy in her hand, not like the Gizmo 3000. The Gizmo 3000 felt rickety, and unstable in her hands. This would be the first time any elf would attempt to power on the Gizmo 4000. It was about to enter field trials. She turned the chrome dials and could hear a distant humming coming from the motor. Once she turned it on, and flipped the switch, there would be no turning back. The heat from the Gizmo 4000's core and aux power made the room smell like Candy Canes. She tried to ignore her sense of dread, but this was now not the time for any failure. Santa and Luigi's Toy Emporium were counting on her.

Before she flipped the power converter on, she removed her hat and looked at her Magic Christmas Bulb. She could do this. Santa chose her and right now it was evident what she had to do. She knew Santa would be busy up in the North Pole getting the last minute preparations done to start the countdown to Christmas Eve. It was almost Midnight. In a few minutes it would be Black Friday, and the rush would be on in the North Pole to ramp up overtime and the mad race would begin to meet the quota of toys. Black Friday was nothing new to the North Pole, in fact Black Friday got its start in the North Pole. Things were by far more frantic in the North Pole than they were in the Lower Latitudes. The elves had millions of toys to prepare for Santa's Sleigh, and each year they had a sharp deadline to keep.

She had a very tall order to fill before the sun came up on the morning of Black Friday. Black Friday was the busiest shopping day of the year, and Santa briefed Lulu on his plan. After the sun came up, and Florida Giuseppe returned to open her store, the shelves would be full of Imaginarium Wands. She would also be surprised to see an unexpected TV promo airing on TVs throughout the country. There was only one store stocked with Imaginarium Wands. Lulu would build enough Imaginarium Wands overnight to meet the coming demand, and with an affordable price point for all, it would still enable Giuseppe's Toy Emporium to prosper once again.

Once Lulu finished, and packed up the Gizmo 4000, Santa asked Lulu to leave this note behind:

"From the North Pole, our gift to you Merry Christmas! S.C."

Little did Florida Giuseppe know, on her behalf, Santa Claus prearranged a TV ad campaign. At no cost to her, because it was a gift from Santa. Once you made a friend in Santa, he would never forget.

Santa knew the phones would ring off the hook, and parents would come to Giuseppe's Toy Emporium in search of the Imaginarium Wand. There would be such a buzz, and demand, Florida Giuseppe would have to limit one per house. Long after the Christmas Season, Salvador Giuseppe's daughter would still see demand for the Imaginarium Wand, and every Black Friday, Santa would bring Lulu Jingle back to restock the shelves with the Imaginarium Wand.

...But for now, Lulu had to get to work.

There was one last toggle switch on the Upper Aux Power to enable the Lower Aux Power to send the "GO TIME" signal to the Gizmo 4000 main bus unit. Lulu swallowed and started singing Christmas Carols as loud as she could.

She flipped the toggle switch, and anticipated something to happen, but there was a brief pause. Lulu looked at the Gizmo 4000 and shook it briefly.

Suddenly there was a bright flash as the Gizmo 4000 roared to life with the power of 4000 working elves. It sparked Christmas Cheer, and through the roar of the main power core, Lulu could hear the sound of Santa's Sleigh Bells. The Gizmo 4000 wanted to fly through the ceiling and beyond, but Lulu controlled it. The Gizmo 4000 had found its match in the nature of Lulu Jingle's Christmas Spirit. The Gizmo 4000 had roared from paper, without field trials and into her hands. The engineers in the North Pole were convinced it wouldn't work. The Gizmo 4000 was much too powerful for any one elf to contain. The elves could manage 3000 working elf hours in one unit, but 4000 was always considered critical mass.

Lulu focused on the beam of brilliant Christmas energy as it whistled, and zapped around like a cosmic torch. She'd memorized the specs for the Imaginarium Wand as the Gizmo 4000 roared in her gloved hands. She flipped the *"Production Engagement"* button and the Gizmo 4000 began crafting the Imaginarium Wand at the pace of 4000 elves working per hour.

Lulu sang merrily as she guided her Gizmo along. Despite the listed 4000 capacity, she was shocked, and excited to see her Gizmo exceed the listed 4000 elf per hour pace. Lulu kept a close eye on the displays in her goggles, and thought to herself, *"This is truly astounding! The Gizmo 4000 is exceeding 4000, but that was only in theory, because this is technically field trials and we had no real data to go off, until now, but no matter, Santa will be pleased when I report back!"*

Her goggles glowed from the reflection of the white beam of Christmas Cheer as Imaginarium Wands began flying out of the Sparkling Beam of light. There was a whirlwind of commotion as if a miniature tornado were whirling, and swirling around Giuseppe's Toy Emporium, but despite the energy of more than 4000 elves working per hour, barely anyone noticed as people continued to walk past the Toy Emporium.

Jingles glanced back, and saw Imaginarium Wands fly from the spinning, whirling, quantum light of Christmas Cheer. All the cat could do was shake his head, if he weren't witnessing this, he would be hard pressed to believe any of it: *an elf from the North Pole was here in this toy store, with some strange beam of light, spitting out thousands of magic wand looking things, while the sound of Sleigh bells filled the room, and no matter how many wands soared from the light, there was still room left on the shelf, but he had to remind himself...this was New York! Oh and lest he forget, he could also speak out loud to this elf, and apparently he spoke with a French Quebec accent.*

As the clock hands traversed the clock on the wall, and time passed, and the morning sun was at hand, Lulu finished the last Imaginarium Wand.

Black Friday

With the morning sun, Lulu waited for the Gizmo 4000 to cool off before she put it back in the old bag Santa had given her before she left the North Pole. The toy store smelled like candy canes, and warm sugar cookies, but there was little she could do about the smell. As soon as Florida Giuseppe arrived at her business to open, there would be no denying, something amazing had happened overnight, so the smell of warm Christmas Cookies, and Cinnamon would probably feel irrelevant to Florida when she found the wands, and read the note from Santa Claus.

Jingles could feel the heat from his perch at the front of the toy store. He remained at his lookout post all night, and kept a watchful eye on the front of the store, just in case, but no one noticed Giuseppe's Toy Emporium, but that was about to change when Florida Giuseppe opened her doors for business.

Jingles stretched with fatigue and jumped down. The streets were quiet, but it would all change as people flooded the streets once more and started their Christmas Shopping. The taxis, buses would again bustle and hustle their fares around the city, but for the moment, it was quiet once again in Giuseppe's Toy Emporium.

Jingles admired the rows of Imaginarium Wands as he strolled to the back of the store to find Lulu.

"Amazing," he said.

Lulu nodded. She was tired, but relieved she'd successfully delivered the Imaginarium Wand in time for Christmas. She knew things were hectic back at the North Pole, and though her face was partially covered in soot, ash, and a little red from the brilliant light and heat, she smiled at Jingles.

"You okay kid? You look a little peaked to be honest."

Lulu removed a handkerchief from her coat pocket and wiped her face clean. She must have looked like she'd spent the night cleaning chimneys with Stanley Dumbroski.

"I'm a little sore, the Gizmo 4000 really packs a punch, and it took a few thousand Imaginarium Wands for me to get the feel for it, but we did it Jingles!" Lulu replied as she sat down to rest for a brief moment, "With your help, we made enough Imaginarium Wands to help Florida Giuseppe, and with Santa's plan in action right now, we'll rescue Giuseppe's Toy Emporium!"

"You did an amazing thing here for these humans, but I had very little to do with the success of your operation tonight Lulu" Jingles said as he surveyed the shelves.

"'We' did it together, because I couldn't have done it without you Jingles."

"We make a good team, don't we?" Jingles said as he purred with approval.

"We sure do Jingles, but now we have to clean the mess up."

"That's easy, just use that Gadget 4000 of yours, and clean up should be a snap."

"It's the Gizmo 4000, but it doesn't work that way Jingles," Lulu laughed, "The Gizmo 4000 can only build toys, but eureka! I do have a nifty trick so we can get clean up done lickety-split," Lulu said as she wiggled her nose, snapped her finger, and blew Santa's Christmas Dust over the piles of tinsel dust, and before Jingles could say a word, the room before them was left sparkling clean. The lingering dust from yesterday, and the day before, in long forgotten shelf space in a never used storage room, was wiped clean and left spring fresh.

"Wow! That was amazing!" Jingles laughed as he admired his sudden fresh coat of fur, "I do believe whatever you did, cleaned me too."

Lulu laughed, "You do smell a little better my friend."

"Well, in my defense, when you spend your life foraging in trash cans for a bite to eat, and though I can score good eats down in the trash cans in Little Italy, it does leave behind a certain odor, but it feels good to no longer smell like three day old Risotto and fish."

There were sparkling Christmas lights swirling around in the residual energy of the cleaning magic Lulu unleashed to tidy up after the Gizmo 4000 turned out an infinite number of Imaginarium Wands. Eventually the twinkling Christmas lights faded, leaving Lulu and Jingles alone under the dim, overnight lighting of Giuseppe's Toy Emporium.

"This whole night has been amazing, even for a stray cat like myself having to hustle on the streets of this town."

"Maybe you're not a stray anymore Jingles? Santa says we all have a purpose, and I think tonight you found yours," Lulu said as she took her pink elf hat on, and put it on Jingles.

It was big on his head and he played with it, until it sat at an angle he could see from it, "It's a little big on me, but I like it. Do you really mean that Lulu?"

"I do Jingles, I know Santa, and if you're interested in coming back to the North Pole with us, I think you'd really like it, and I can use your help again on future missions."

There was a residual air of magic in the room. It felt electric to Lulu and Jingles. The toy store smelled like warm Christmas cookies and fruit cake.

"What's that smell Lulu?" Jingles asked.

"Jingles, that's the smell of magic!"

"I like it," Jingles said.

"Get used to it, but more importantly than magic Jingles is our Christmas Spirit, and I can tell you have it."

"I do? I never thought I did. I never got a gift from Santa, and cats have a reputation you know?"

"You gave tonight Jingles, you shared your time, and shared concern for Florida Giuseppe. You gave a gift tonight, Jingles, and that's more important than magic." Jingles sat quietly and felt humbled by what he'd seen and the warm invitation back to the North Pole with his new friend. "I would like for you to keep my Christmas Bulb. It's your promise now, the same one Santa gave me."

"I don't know what to say Lulu."

"It's Black Friday Jingles, and back home it's the start of the Christmas Season and things are very hectic now, so let's just say, 'Merry Christmas' to one another and head upstairs to the roof and wait for Santa to pick us up. I know he'll be so happy to meet you, and hear all about how you helped me tonight!"

"Well let me be the first to wish you a, 'Merry Christmas Lulu Jingle!'"

"Merry Christmas Jingles!"

Lulu knew it was organized chaos back at the North Pole. Elf City would bustle with traffic. Santa's Workshop would be on overtime now until Christmas Eve. It was starting to snow on the roof of the toy store as Lulu and

Jingles waited for Santa's sleigh. Each snowflake shimmered like an ornament on a Christmas tree as it fell.

Though the sun was starting to break over the horizon, and because the first snow of Christmas was starting to fall it felt enchanting to many, and though it felt inviting, and filled many with the anticipation for Christmas morning, no one took a moment to glance up, but if they had, they would have seen Santa's sleigh, and eight tiny reindeer carry Lulu Jingle and the newest resident of the North Pole back home.

What Happened Next...

Florida Giuseppe was much too busy to turn on her television or radio when she woke up on Black Friday. It was the busiest shopping day of the season, but not for her store. It was over, this would be the last Christmas her father's store would be open she thought glumly as she headed out to open her doors for business. As much as she missed her father, she was glad he wasn't around to see it.

...because she was too busy with her morning, and leaving home to open her store, Florida Giuseppe never saw the commercials splashed all over the television, nor heard the radio spots, guiding many shoppers to her toy store.

Though she never purchased an ad for her store, because there was never any money in the budget for expensive advertisement, her toy store was getting prime exposure in homes all over.

Florida was unaware there were parents all over the city, clamoring to get to Giuseppe's Toy Emporium so they could be the first to purchase the Imaginarium Wand. There would be no need for parents to feel anxious Giuseppe's Toy Emporium would run out of wands, because Lulu and Jingles made enough for all, but Santa wanted the marketing buzz to drive parents towards the store. The whimsical new toy was catching like a wildfire in the hearts, and imaginations in children all around the city, and in no time, Giuseppe's Toy Emporium was the place to shop for Christmas! In no time, Giuseppe's Toy Emporium went viral on the internet and crashed the store's website with order requests. All of this marketing buzz, and growing demand caught on before Florida Giuseppe arrived to open the store for business.

The Imaginarium Wand appeared differently to each child as they watched on tv. The Imaginarium Wand could be anything a child wanted to play and just make believe. No wand was the same, and even parents felt their inner child stir as they smiled, and remembered what it felt like to play, *"let's pretend and make believe."*

The phone at Giuseppe's Toy Emporium wouldn't stop ringing as hundreds called. Buses started bringing shoppers down to the darkened store as a line started to form outside. Taxis dropped parents off, and much to many parents' dismay, they had to find the end of the line as it started to grow around the block, and beyond. Other parents jumped on line and started to look to familiar larger online retailers, but felt frustration when they realized they could only buy the much sought after Imaginarium Wand through this one, and only authorized store in New York City. Santa was clever, he never forgets his friends, and Santa would always be grateful to Salvador Giuseppe and his family. He knew the Imaginarium Wand would help children restore the joy of *make believe* and create unlimited hours of play with their imaginations, at the same time, help his friends. With the help of Lulu Jingle, and Jingles the cat, there were an infinite number of Imaginarium Wands to go around. Even if a parent couldn't get a wand under their tree for that Christmas morning, and because shipping out that many Imaginarium Wands could pose a logistical headache for the post office, and overnight delivery services, there was next Christmas, or if someone took the time to come visit Giuseppe's Toy Emporium after Christmas, they could also buy one for their home.

As Florida walked towards her store she had to wade her way through a line that went in the direction of her toy store.

"What's the hold up?" she heard someone ask.

"I don't think they're open yet," someone answered.

Well this is odd Florida thought as she continued to excuse herself through the crowd. She didn't understand why so many people were milling about on her store's avenue. She looked up twice at the street signs, just to make sure she wasn't absent minded in her thinking as she stepped off the subway earlier. She was feeling sad, and melancholy that morning, so it would be understandable.

"Nope, this is the right avenue," she said quietly as the snow continued to fall, and blanket the sidewalk. Yellow Taxi cabs were passing her regularly, and appeared to stop in front of her store. There was an excited buzz in the air as it mingled with the first snow of the new Christmas season. The line was indeed headed towards her front door.

"Excuse me folks," Florida asked as she tried to wade through the line of people looking through her store's window.

"How come we've never been here before?" a bystander asked the person standing next to her.

"I'm not sure hunny, but we're gonna tell others to come check out Giuseppe's Toy Emporium," the bystander responded as they waited in the long line.

"What's going on here?" Florida asked another as they waited patiently for her to open her store, but before they could respond, an angry voice yelled from somewhere behind her, *"Hey lady, the line starts back up the street somewhere, you'll have to wait like the rest of us for Giuseppe's Toy Emporium to open up!"*

"Oh I apologize, I appreciate everyone's patience, I'm Florida Giuseppe, and this is my store, I'll be opening momentarily."

Florida saw the angry man as he waited in the cold, but when he saw Florida, his expression turned patient, "Oh Miss, I apologize but we've been waiting outside for awhile, but we're all very excited to come inside and start our Christmas shopping in your store."

Florida wanted to pinch her cheeks to see if she were dreaming all of this, but there was no need to pinch her cheeks, because they were already stinging from the falling snow.

"Oh wait, this is your store?" Another bystander asked.

"Yes, I'm Florida Giuseppe, and my father opened this store in 1939. I'm a second generation toy store proprietor."

"Merry Christmas Miss Giuseppe!" Someone cried out to her from far back in the line, as word was passed down, *"Florida Giuseppe was here!"*

The grumpy man stuck his hand out to shake Florida's hand.

"I'm happy we could bring you our business today Miss Giuseppe, the advertisement said we should ask for you."

Florida was now more confused than ever, but she could at least open her toy store, and invite everyone inside. She would make hot chocolate like her father once did, and play Christmas music.

Word was passed down the long line Giuseppe's Toy Emporium was going to open shortly.

It was really starting to snow, and Florida was getting cold, but as she started to unlock her store's front door, she saw the reflection of a tall, distinguished, well dressed older gentleman tilt his hat in a greeting towards her.

Florida looked stunned as she turned around.

"Merry Christmas Florida Giuseppe. There's a note inside explaining it all."

"Okay..." Florida stammered as she recognized the long white beard, sparkling blue eyes.

"I will never forget my friend Florida, and Salvador was both a good man, and a good friend of mine."

"Merry Christmas to you as well Sir," Florida whispered as she shook his hand, and though she was baffled by it all, and perhaps a little uncertain as to the identity of the distinguished gentleman, she was starting to understand as she reflected on the many stories her father shared with her about Santa Claus as she was growing up.

The gentleman smiled knowingly at her, and asked, "What time do you open today? It appears you have a very large crowd of eager shoppers..."

"Now...I'm open now," Florida stammered as she fumbled with the keys again.

"Splendid! Oh by the way, I'm from out of town, but I've been here a time or two. Do you think you could point this 'tourist' in the right direction to Central Park? The park is lovely in the snow, wouldn't you agree? I think I'd like to take a walk over there before I head back home."

Before Florida could answer the tall, distinguished, well dressed gentleman with a flowing white beard in the direction of Central Park, he smiled, tipped his hat once more, and walked away through the large crowd. Once she lost sight of him in the crowd of eager shoppers, Florida unlocked the doors to her store.

Once inside, she turned on the lights, and saw the shelves stocked with a whimsical looking wand. As promised, she saw the note, and she knew it would explain it all to her, but there was no time, because she was suddenly busy with shoppers.

"Merry Christmas!" Customers said as they came inside, and out of the snow and cold.

"Merry Christmas Everyone! Giuseppe's Toy Emporium is open for business!"

This is the end of the story for now, but until we hear once again from the North Pole, Lulu Jingle would like to wish everyone...
Merry Christmas!

About this Author:

I reside in Solomons Maryland. In the corner of Southern Maryland, next to the beautiful Chesapeake Bay I live with my girlfriend Robin, and our two dogs. I started writing when I was in highschool, but forgot my love for writing until 2012, when I wrote my first story, "When an Angel Intervenes." Though the story is written as a fiction, it was based on a true story. Writing "When an Angel Intervenes" and remembering those things from my childhood, is why I became a suicide awareness advocate. Telling my story was difficult at times, and a challenge, but opened the gate towards healing, helping others, and taught me to write once again.

I don't plan out my stories or outline them in advance, because where's the fun in that? I follow the characters as they progress through the story, and they're often inspired by an idea. I jot down in my notes a sentence or two about the inspiration, and leave it there, until I feel compelled to tell the story. Sometimes, my inspiration comes from a story title, as in the case of Lulu Jingle. Lulu Jingle was born from a title only, but Lulu took it from there. I know we've not heard the last from Lulu, she's an independent elf who recently discovered her purpose in the North Pole.

Bonus Story

Because it's Christmas!

The
Little Slugger
by
Jim Atkisson

Copyright
2024

Hebrews 11:1

The King James Bible

"Now faith is the substance of things hoped for, the evidence of things not seen."

the beginning;

Twenty five years after life on McCutchen Lane, I heard through the grapevine one of my friends passed. Jonah Martz left this world the same age his mom did. When someone passed on the news to me, it really took me back to that time in life. It all felt so fresh to me. The memories came flooding back to me, and because I didn't have to go digging for them, it felt like the summer of 1980 for that day as I processed the news about the passing of *The Little Slugger*.

If you have a half hour to sit with me while I eat lunch, I'll pour us a cup of coffee and tell you the story about the Little Slugger and a little about Big Valley City and its park.

Remember when you were a kid? Remember when things were easier to believe in? Santa Claus, the Easter Bunny, Shooting Stars, were concepts we just accepted like gravity back then. Faith was in no short supply back in those days, but as we all got a little older, a little more cynical, jaded, faith became a challenge. Birthday wishes, we all made them before we blew out our birthday candles, and we believed if we made a wish, our wish would come true, but today? Now? It all feels like a formality we follow through before we eat the birthday cake someone prepared for us.

I was there on that hot summer day. The day Jonah Martz became *the* Little Slugger of Big Valley and a living legend before he turned eleven years old. We all played on the same baseball team that summer, and all of us had nicknames like mobsters have within the rank and file of their gang. Before Jonah became the Little Slugger in legend, he was known as the Little Slugger to his mom and dad, and on this particular day, the Big Valley BobCats were invited over to Jonah's house for cake and ice cream and to celebrate Jonah's birthday.

Though it was Jonah's day, he was feeling very sad on that particular day. Though I'd not seen or spoken to Jonah in years, I could still see the moment he cracked that glorious grand slam out of the park. I could still hear the crack of the bat and it was a beautiful sound.

The summer of 1980 and life on McCutchen Lane was a good time to be a ten year old and call McCutchen Lane our home. You had to have faith to believe, to believe in the things you can't see, or hear, much less feel. I don't want to sound like I'm railing against today's kids, but I do feel sorry for them, because in my opinion they're losing that *hard-wired* child-like faith that came so naturally once upon a time. Remember those *once-upon-a-time* bedtime stories our parents used to read? Today's kids are exposed to what's on the internet and seem to have lost the spark of their own imaginations. They might be ten in years, but because they're inundated with information from the internet that others create, they're aging within their imagination. If dogs age seven years for every human year, from what I've seen, the internet is aging today's kid's ability to believe in the impossible. Maybe there's no such thing as the Easter Bunny, but back when we were seven years old, the majority of us believed in the Easter Bunny, but today a kid can do a quick internet search and see for themselves. Faith is muscle and if you don't use it, you lose it and become cynical and jaded.

Why does it really matter? When we're faith centered people, we have a tendency to be a little kinder towards others. We all seem to have fewer health problems, live with fewer regrets, and have a tendency to see little miracles around us daily. Storms do happen in life, and we all need faith to pass through life's storms.

The baseball field was the place for us to spend our summers, but more specifically, the place to be was in the heart of Big Valley City at the Big Valley City Park. If you've never been to Big Valley City, and never heard about the park, the best way I could describe the whole experience would be to compare it to New York City's Central Park, but on a smaller scale. If the Emerald City, inside of the Kingdom of Oz had a city park, it would feel like the park in Big Valley. It was an enchanted place to spend a summer day or night. There was magic in that park, and when it was fueled by the imagination and faith of a kid in the summer of 1980, anything could happen. There was a lot for us to do. Before the internet and cellphones we spent time sailing our model ships across the park's lake, canoeing, and skipping rocks from the pier. We meandered and explored the miles of paths that curved and twisted through the park. We honestly felt we were inside of the realm of an enchanted kingdom inside of the park's marble ornate walls. In the winter we ice skated, and played hockey over the frozen lake. No matter the time of the year, there was always life in Big Valley's own Central Park, but the real attraction to the park was the spectacle on Ferris Island. Ferris Island was a small island in the middle of the lake.

The city founders and architects like most planners wanted their city to prosper and entice people to do business, live, and raise their families. They wanted tourism and it was vital for the city to become a destination city. The city was at a disadvantage compared to the rest of the cities within the state, because of where Big Valley was located on the map. Big Valley was planted hundreds of miles away from the state capital and other neighboring cities. In fact, there were no neighboring cities, just miles of mountain ridges, forests and shadow filled valleys. Despite what the state legislators promised and impact studies the city planners and architects knew there was little reason for anyone to travel to the lone city on the other side of the state, unless they did something to bring people to Big Valley. The city planners took many trips to New York city to walk its streets and studied how the city became the financial capital of the world. One such trip local Big Valley investors and city planners noticed the Statue of Liberty and felt inspired to build their own Statue of Liberty on Ferris Island. Like everything else inside of the park it would be scaled down, and it would be an expensive project, funded by private money, donated to the city, it could be done. The planners turned to Brighton Savage Senior, the owner and founder of Savage Quality Tires for help.

I know it sounds like I'm wandering, and I only have my lunch break to reflect on what happened back then, because I started telling the story about the Little Slugger, but every play needs a stage, and every stage needs a backdrop. This was how things were back in August of '80.

Jonah Martz moved with his dad and grandparents to McCutchen lane that year. Savage Quality Tires was the biggest employer in the state, one of the top employers on the East Coast. Times were good in the city, and just as the city planners and architects planned for, families were flocking to the city. Annually employment was up and crime was down. It was also a pivotal summer for myself and most of my friends. We noticed girls for the first time at the swimming pool. Maybe we'd noticed them the previous summers, but now we were all willing to admit it to one another. Suddenly girls were no longer something to feel compelled to abhor, shiver over if heaven forbid one of them showed us any attention, or acted like they may actually *"like"* one of us, because there would come a day a few years in the future we'd given up pizza, or TV for that same attention. Though we still watched Saturday morning cartoons we were also growing into more *cool and adult* novelties. Bobby *Curveball* Mackee stole his older brother's pack of cigarettes and we all tried out our first smoke that summer. Well out of sight from anyone who might know us, we lit up and felt stricken with the consequences. We decided Saturday morning cartoons were still cool and smoking was better left to the more sophisticated teenagers and our parents. Sadly, we were unknowing, losing the gift of a *childlike faith* and to believe without question.

The tire company was experiencing another record breaking year and families were still pouring into the city in search of the American Dream in Big Valley City. While the rest of the country was experiencing a recession during the Jimmy Carter Presidency, Big Valley became the bright shining light on the hill to the rest of the state. I'll say it again, things were very good in Big Valley when *Jonah, The Little Slugger-Martz* moved to Big Valley with his family.

Brighton Savage Senior was a visionary. He was the owner of multiple patents and the CEO for Savage Quality Tires. He was unmatched in his commitment to customer service and quality. His tires were ahead of their time. Mr. Savage stood by every tire, without exception that rolled out of his plant, and onto every car, or truck. It was his name on those tires and he took a personal interest in what his customers were saying about his tires. He was a pioneer in tires and strived to focus on quality and let the tires speak for themselves in the marketplace. A marketplace that at the time was dominated by larger, less personal conglomerates.

Brighton's motto and ad campaign was simple, "They told me to not reinvent the wheel, so we decided to be the one who put the tire on the wheel." It was a simple message, and he was unwavering in quality. It was widely known his tires were more expensive, because he believed in passing on the profits to the people who made the tires and to the city those people called their home. Savage Quality Tires was a private company, never public on any of the exchanges, and as time went on, became a target for the larger conglomerates. The sharks noticed what was happening in Big Valley and the upstart younger, smaller company and their shrinking market shares. Something had to be done, so instead of improving their business models and products, the larger companies set out to take out Savage Quality Tires.

However, because this is a story about Jonah. A story about baseball, and faith, I'll save that story for another time.

Like I say, families were flocking into Big Valley, especially that summer. The city was bursting at the seams with prosperity and growth. New home construction was in hot demand and any available home for sale was under a contract the same day it went up for sale.

McCutcheon Lane was lined with red brick homes, tidy flower beds, and manicured lawns. The streets were shaded by proud Oak and Maple trees. Though my friends and I enjoyed the good life on McCutcheon, we all lived within sight of the ominous shadows of the Savage Tire plant's enormous brick smokestacks. From our front porch the stacks appeared to stand over the city landscape like a towering escarpment. Though they were eerie at times, particularly during foggy nights, there was a reassuring sense that came from their presence as they loomed over our homes and neighborhoods. As long as there was a lazy thin ribbon of blue industrial smoke wafting towards the sky by day, and the smell of rubber by night, there was a prevailing sense everything remained normal in our city. There were strobe lights etched into the side of the massive brick smokestacks. Day and night, seven days a week, year round, white lights by day, and red flashing lights by night, spelled, "SAVAGE TIRE." As long as the smoke smelled like rubber and the twinkling lights continued to flash the name of our benefactor the city would continue to enjoy lavish prosperity. If the tires were the lifeblood and the manufacturing plant was the heart...*the city park was the soul of the city.*

During that summer I played first base for the BobCats. In fact, most of my friends on McCutchen Lane played for the BobCats. The BobCats were a notorious team within little league baseball circles. Our Bobcats had an unmatched losing streak. The Bobcats for whatever reason, were never able to pull off a win and the year Jonah Martz moved to McCutcheon Lane with his father and grandparents was pretty much another losing season for the BobCats. Teams came to the Big Valley City Park, ball field C, to break their own losing streaks, because our Bobcats would most certainly lose to a visiting team. The Big Valley City Park had seven little league baseball fields. Ball field C, was the technical *"home"* field for the Bobcats. We shared the park with seven other little league teams, and kids who lived in and around our neighborhood played for the Bobcats.

Eddie Martz moved his family into 8073 McCutcheon Avenue on the 3rd anniversary of his wife's death. Judith Martz left this world after a brief, but heroic battle with an aggressive illness. Jonah Martz was seven years old when his mom left this world. When I met him a few years later, her passing was still affecting my new friend, but having never lost a parent at the time, it was hard for myself and the rest of us to relate to him, but we all tried to be good friends for the new kid on McCutcheon Lane.

Eddie Martz moved to Big Valley from the other side of the state after he went to a career fair near the state capital and got hired on the spot. Eddie Martz was a veteran of the Vietnam War and a purple heart recipient and an excellent fit for Savage Tire. Mr. Martz also brought his parents to Big Valley to help him raise Jonah. He was a widower at the age of thirty and dealing with the scars of war at the same time he was trying to care for his grieving nine year old. There was a lot of sadness on 8073 McCutcheon Avenue after they moved on, but it did not deter the BobCats from welcoming the new kid into their dugout as one of their own.

Gosh...how could I forget to introduce myself?

But, I can tell you I was there the day The Little Slugger hit the greatest grand slam Big Valley City Park ever saw.

My name is Jake Parker, but my friends called me Fastball Parker.

Jonah became a legend when he snapped the longest losing streak on record and he did it on his birthday. We all watched in wonder and disbelief as the white, leather ball flew far into the sky. Parents, players, and umpire watched Jonah's ball soar towards the park's Statue of Liberty before it vanished from sight. We were eyewitnesses to history and the power of faith and imagination that afternoon. No one said a word as the Little Slugger jogged towards first base. The only sound that anyone could hear was the sound of the bees buzzing around the baseball field. It was only when Jonah started towards second base did the vibe change into a big outburst of excitement and celebrating. It was quite a moment.

Did I mention the bees? There were quite a few and it was only when Jonah crossed home plate did things take a very dire, and unexpected turn.

It was a bad turn, but it was a day of miracles and things do have a way of working out in God's time.

I've said a lot about the park, but it was a place for the inexplicable and if you take the seed of unwavering faith, a birthday wish, and plant it all in that enchanted park, things would happen. Inside of those marble and iron fences, decorated with bronze gates, it was darn right magical most days. I'm not sure why it felt that way, but anyone from Big Valley City knew it. Maybe the place was established over some mystical Ley Lines if you believe in that sort of thing, but no matter, for whatever reason our park was one unique place to spend time inside of.

With that said, it should be of little surprise when little Jonah Martz crushed that baseball so far outside of the park, legendary Reggie Jackson was said to have called Jonah Martz to congratulate him and wish him, "Happy Birthday." I can only speculate if that part of the story was rumored or fact, but the rest of this tale was fact. Personally, I like to believe he called him on his birthday, because he was Jonah's favorite baseball player at the time and it would have meant a lot to us.

Aside from the replica Statue of Liberty and seven baseball fields there were numerous soccer fields, and basketball courts. There were rolling hills for kids to roll down during the summer and slide down during the winter months. There were frisbee tournaments, dog parks, and many marriage proposals. There was always the smell of fresh cut grass, hot pretzels, hot peanuts, and popcorn from the many food vendors. The park was the premier place to come watch the 4th of July fireworks and no matter how much of the park you explored, there was always a new path leading to some undiscovered part of the park. Maybe it was part of the mystique of our park, it never really had a beginning or an end.

There is much to say about the park, but one more detail about our park, it was the home of the Big Valley City Badgers. Highschool football is a religion in Big Valley City, with traditions running deep. If it weren't for those boys, Big Valley City would not have survived the economic downturn that would eventually come for our city. Remember those tire conglomerates? Those kids rallied our city at our darkest hour and brought it back from ruin, but another story, for another time.

make a wish;

"*Jonah?*" Eddie Martz said softly, tapping on his son's bedroom door. This was his third try at getting Jonah to come downstairs and enjoy his birthday. It was his day, a birthday milestone, but though his son should be happy, he wasn't and though he was sad, it was understandable. He was grieving a loss.

Three years ago today, his mom passed from this life. Judy Martz passed from this life onto the next, on Jonah's seventh birthday. His birthday would now always be an anniversary. Another year, another year to remember the day she lost her painful battle with the disease that took her from her family. Eddie missed the love of his life, today was extra bitter for him, but right now he needed to be there for his boy. He knew Jonah was grieving, but he knew Judy would want her son to live the day and celebrate with his new neighborhood friends.

"Jonah, buddy can you come downstairs? Your friends are on their way over and should be here soon." He waited for a response, but stood and looked at a silent, closed door. "Your presents are downstairs waiting for you..."

The notion of presents, cake, and ice cream sounded foreign to Jonah. Another time, another kid, but not him. He didn't want to acknowledge today, but everyone insisted he had his party today, complete with cake, and birthday candles. He was miserable and he wanted to be left alone in his room. The idea of crawling under the covers and pillows was more appealing than the circus going on downstairs.

His heart ached once more. His face burned and stung from the tears.

He missed his mom.

She was dead.

Deceased.

"She fought and she was so brave..."

Meaningless words. They always said she was so brave, and fought. Jonah knew better how much she fought the disease. He didn't want anyone to tell him this, they were stepping into his private memories of his mom and he missed her so much.

Cake?

Presents?

"...make a wish and blow out the candles Jonah," someone would say.

He was the only kid he knew who had to accept his mom was dead.

Some kids' moms and dads were divorced, but this was different. She was gone. Not gone for a little awhile, but gone permanently.

She died on his birthday. He didn't understand the word *"unfortunate irony"* because he heard the adults whisper the word *"irony"* as defined by Webster, but he knew what this word felt like.

He didn't want to play baseball today and didn't care if the BobCats lost their last game of the season. They were going to lose anyway, so why put the energy in trying today? He knew was thinking like a *"Rotten Egg"* but so what? Birthdays and baseball were for the living, not the dead.

"...besides all this crummy city cares about is football."

He was homesick for his old neighborhood. He hated living in the valley, behind the mountains, far from the rest of the cities in the state, and far from his old friends.

Baseball was a low priority in Big Valley City. Even the annoying real estate agent who showed his dad around the city wasted no time asking him if he played football? It would make little difference in today's outcome if Jonah showed up or stayed home. They would lose with him, and lose if he stayed home.

He looked at the picture of his mom on his bedroom wall. It was his favorite picture of her, taken before she was diagnosed with the disease. It was a happier time and back when things were normal.

"It's not fair." he thought as he wiped away the tears. They were the worst, because it hurt his face and he really didn't have more.

He could hear other kids playing in the street outside. They were lucky, they weren't stuck in this nightmare.

Jonah felt a wave of guilt. He knew his thinking was rotten, "rotten like an egg."

His mom said he had to be brave. He could remember the talks they had. He promised to be brave, and he wasn't feeling very brave right now.

The BobCats needed everyone today. It was their last chance to end the losing streak. If they lost today, it would mean another season, without a win in the win column. Another shut-out season for field seven.

"Wasn't the number seven supposed to be a lucky number?" Jonah muttered as he picked up his glove and tossed a worn baseball into it.

Jonah was the new kid on McCutcheon Lane, but the kids on the BobCats were friendly, and accepting to the newcomer. They were really cool at times, and they did make him laugh sometimes, especially when laughing seemed so hard for him to do. He felt a little guilty for missing his old friends, because his new friends were pretty cool to play baseball with and ride bikes up and down McCutcheon Lane.

Jonah could hear his grandmother come up the stairs, and stop just outside of his bedroom door.

Muffled voices.

"He needs a therapist Edward..."

"No he doesn't. He just needs more time mom..."

He loved his grandmother, but he knew she just didn't get it, or really understand.

"I don't need a therapist, that's a dumb idea," he thought. "I need to see her. I wish my mom were here today. That's what I need, not a dumb therapist."

He felt as if he were on display today. A weird novelty. A show-n-tell exhibit the other kids and teachers were gawking at. He didn't like the whispering.

He heard his dad sigh, and head back down stairs. His grandmother was unwilling to give up, and let her grandson miss his birthday. She was persistent with him.

"Jonah?" She tapped softly on his bedroom door. "Honey, I know today is hard, but sometimes the hardest days in life turn out to be the days we find the most happiness. She loved you son, you were her world Jonah."

He felt the tears again. His eyes burned from them and he suddenly decided going downstairs would be better than more crying. He'd stop crying in front of the BobCats. He wouldn't allow them to see that. His friends were coming over to cheer him up and get ready for their last game of the season. It was no secret, Jonah's mom was dead, and she died on *his* birthday. There were

365 days in a year. His mom died on the day he was supposed to remember the day he was born and every year he was supposed to remember the day he was born, he would remember it was also the day his mom left him.

"I'll be downstairs in a minute," he said flatly, much to her surprise. Though he couldn't see her through the door, he could feel her relief.

Jonah was only ten, but he was growing up fast. He'd learned the adults were uncomfortable with grief, and they seemed to push him along on his own journey without the person who gave life to him. They often told him his mom lived in his heart, as if that was supposed to make it better. He heard his mom's voice sometimes, but she wasn't there when he learned to ride the bike. She wasn't there to cut the crusts from his peanut and butter sandwiches. His dad left the crusts on the bread, but not because he wouldn't cut the crusts from the bread, he didn't know Jonah hated the crusts and would just pull the crust off himself. This was something that belonged to his mom. Something she did for him everyday, and no one could replace this. Jonah didn't want anyone to cut the crusts from his bread, ever.

"Little Slugger, I'm so happy you're going downstairs," she said. Jonah recognized his mom's voice from inside of his intuition. He couldn't hear her with his ears, but he *could* hear her with his heart. Maybe people do live on in our hearts.

"Mom?" He wouldn't speak it. He only imagined he spoke back to her, because he didn't want anyone to say he needed to go see a therapist.

"Chin up today Little Slugger, no more tears today."

Jonah wiped his face.

"I am proud of you baby. I know you hear it often since I had to leave, but you're a very brave Little Slugger."

The room was empty, but there was an intuitive connection that crossed time and space.

"Don't forget your birthday wish today," she reminded him from her place in heaven.

"I won't forget my wish mom," he whispered back.

He couldn't forget his wish. He had one shot at wishing for anything he wanted. Ten burning candles. Ten burning birthday candles held an intrinsic magic, but only if he believed in what he wished for. That was the caveat, and stipulation to any birthday wish. Easy to remember, but hard to do. If he wanted his wish to come true, he had to remember the fine print. Today was the day for a wish to come true, and there was no limit on what he could wish for. He could only have one wish, but he could wish for anything...

"Jonah, are you okay?" his grandmother said.

"I'm fine grandma. I'll be downstairs in a minute, I promise..." he said, forgetting she was still waiting for him just outside of his bedroom door.

"I could hear you talking to someone," she said.

He wiped his face and despite his burning, and swollen eyes, he felt better. Suddenly, Jonah felt hopeful. His birthday wish was like finding twenty dollars in his sock drawer. Overlooked all this time, he had currency right now and something he could use to leverage, but he had to be creative and make sure this wish counted.

"No. I'm not talking to anyone," he said. He picked up his baseball hat and put it on.

"Okay honey, I swore I could've heard you talking to someone, but never mind. I can hear your friends downstairs right now. They'll be excited to see you Jonah."

"I'm happy you're going downstairs Little Slugger, put on a big smile for me."

"Thank you Grandma, I'll be right down."

"Okay Jonah...why don't you take a minute and wash up before you come down. I'll let the BobCats know you're coming down."

Jonah put his baseball glove under his armpit like one of the big leaguers and took a moment to look at his uniform in the mirror. As long as he could remember, probably after Jonah could walk, he loved baseball. When he turned two, his mom got him a plastic bat and ball for his birthday. Judy Martz said her son took to a bat and ball like a fish takes to water.

"You're my Little Slugger..."

The nickname stuck, because as it turned out, Jonah was the smallest boy in his class, and on every baseball team he played on. It didn't matter, because he was The Little Slugger. He imagined he was *the* great Babe Ruth of Little League Baseball, and even before Eddie Martz could unpack his moving truck now parked on McCutcheon Lane, he signed Jonah up to play baseball for the Big Valley BobCats. Jonah found a home on the haphazard, loss-prone BobCats. The team welcomed the new kid with the nickname, because as it turned out, all the BobCats had nicknames and this saved them the trouble of figuring out what to call him.

The biggest fear Jonah lived with; he'd get used to her being gone. Jonah felt a wave of doubt in his ability to make a wish downstairs. Grief was affecting his ability to believe in the things he once believed in so easily, or maybe grief was making him grow up faster than the rest of his friends, because he no longer believed in the same things they did. He knew his friends still believed in Santa Claus, but he didn't believe anymore. He stopped believing in the Easter Bunny years ago. He was sure his friends no longer believed in him, because no one brought it up anymore. Jonah hated the idea of the Easter Bunny now, because that was one more thing he'd never do again with his mom. She used to paint eggs for Jonah and hide them so he could go hunt for them. They always went to church on Easter, but lately Jonah felt himself becoming angry towards God. The older he got, the harder it was to believe in the things he could not see.

"What will you wish for today Little Slugger?" she asked from across the space of eternity.

"I can't tell you, or the wish won't come true..."

"That's right, you remember what the fine print says about making birthday wishes," she said.

How could he forget what the fine print stipulated when it came to making a wish. The rules were immutable. Simple to remember, but very hard to follow, because it required faith to follow. He already had two strikes against him. He no longer believed in the Easter Bunny, and he questioned Santa Claus, and did he still have the faith to believe in the power of a birthday wish? The first stipulation spelled out, *"he had to believe in what he wished for, would come true."* The second rule, *"it has to remain a secret."* Whatever he wished for, would have to remain a secret.

He could wish right now, *"I wish you were at my game today mom,"* but absent the birthday cake, and candles, they were meaningless words. The wish had to be wished for, just prior to blowing out the birthday candles, and only within that sacred space, would the universe honor his wish.

"You have faith Little Slugger, don't doubt what you can do," she said quietly from her place in heaven.

"I don't think I can wish for this mom, because what I want is too big."

"Nothing is impossible when you believe, son."

He could hear her, but he couldn't see her, and he couldn't really hear her with his ears, he could only hear her in his thoughts. It was hard to believe in things he couldn't see, could he really hear his mom? The reality? What he could actually see? She died three years ago today. No kid should have to try and understand death, but some kids do, and some kids die, some kids lose friends, and some kids lose their brother, or sister. The Easter Bunny was easier to accept than try and understand why God took his mom to live in heaven. The cold facts were there before him to accept: there was no Easter Bunny, no Santa Claus, and his mom was dead, and most likely, not really alive in his heart like their priest and his grandma said.

"I love you Little Slugger," she reminded him.

Little Slugger. That was his nickname. His mom loved to come to his games, and no matter how sick her treatments made her, she never missed a game. Out of all the parents in the bleachers, she cheered the loudest for her boy, even the last few weeks of her life, she fought for her boy. She had faith. She was brave for him, and he needed to be brave for her right now. He remembered her grimace from pain at times, and how weak and frail her voice sounded, but she refused to stay at home in the hospice bed. His mom always smiled through the pain.

Today was also the last day to end the historic losing streak. He could wish for a win. It would make his friends happy. He imagined them running from the dugout and onto the field to celebrate their first and only win of the season. A win, was a win, even if it came at the end of the season, it would still be a win for the BobCats. He needed to put Santa behind him, because he needed to be brave like his mom. There were bad things in the world, but there were also good things too. He wanted to see his mom one more time. He had to believe anything was possible, even that.

"You're friends need you Little Slugger."

"I can't mom. I only have one wish. I don't have two, or I'd use one of them for my friends."

"Wouldn't it be exciting to win today Jonah?"

"I can't mom. I have to make this count."

"Helping your friends counts for so much, Little Slugger. There's no greater love than when someone lays down their own life for a friend."

"I can't tell you what I'm going to wish for today mom."

"I know you'll do what's right, because you're very brave Jonah and I know how much you love the BobCats."

Jonah didn't want to have to be brave, just for once, he wanted to be a normal kid, like the ones he could hear riding bikes up and down McCutcheon Lane. They were laughing, and if it weren't for his friends on the BobCats, Jonah would never laugh.

"The BobCats will be fine without my birthday wish," he argued back within the space of his own thoughts.

His mom was close, but he didn't want to admit she could possibly be alive in his heart, in the love they shared. It still wasn't the same, because she wasn't the one waiting for him to come downstairs. He missed her, and there was never a break from missing his mom.

"You're a very thoughtful young man Jonah. I'm sorry you've lost so much, and I know it's a lot to ask of you, but I know you'll put your friends first today."

If he used his birthday wish to benefit his team today, they would never know Jonah sacrificed the time he might have with his mom, so they might for once, break the winless streaking.

"I understand what you're feeling Little Slugger, but most heroes are never in the spotlight, they make those sacrifices while no one else is looking, but I know, and so does God. He understands your heart's desire, and your faith."

"Please don't go..." he almost begged, on the verge of tears again. He was desperate to keep the channel open to her, but he also felt as if he were talking to a breeze, or an empty corner in his bedroom.

He went to the bathroom to wash his face. He felt better after his tear stained face was washed. It was the first time he was out of the bedroom today. Maybe holding up in his bedroom, hesitant to come out and embrace the day, was adding to his sadness. The sunshine felt good on his face and for a moment, he smiled.

He could hear his teammates and friends laughing downstairs.

"It would be nice to win for once," he thought as he stood at the top of the stairs, and readied himself for what happened next.

Though he no longer believed in Santa, he knew there was power in a birthday wish. He just had to believe it was possible, and not doubt it.

"I only have one chance to change things today."

The sound of his friend's laughter warmed his sad heart. He felt another smile. He wanted to see his mom, just once more, but honestly wasn't sure if he could believe that was possible.

"How would she get here? It would be impossible for his mom to come from heaven, but the details weren't up to him, he just had to believe, and the rest would work its way out."

It was an immutable law of nature, like gravity, what goes up, will come down.

One birthday.

Make one wish.

Believe it's possible.

Keep it a secret.

Let the universe take it from there.

Jonah headed downstairs.

He was greeted by a thunderous chorus of cheers and singing. He was hugged on all sides and slapped on the back, no less than seven times.

Most of his baseball team was crowded into the small dining room. There were brightly wrapped presents piled on the dining room table. Jonah felt happy, until he saw his mom's empty chair. It was her place at the dining room table, and if she were there today, she'd be sitting in that spot, smiling at him.

He also saw the birthday cake, ready for him, with ten burning candles. His mom used to always make his cake, now his grandmother made them. He felt sick and started to waver from his decision to use his wish for the benefit of his baseball team. He didn't care, and needed a break from missing his mom. He wanted one more hug from her, just one more. Was that too much to ask of anyone? All he really wanted for his birthday was one more hug from his mom.

"Chin up Little Slugger, remember today is your day," she reassured his broken heart. No one could hear her, but he could.

"I'm sad," he wanted to say out loud, but he couldn't. He had to be brave and be there for everyone, because they had shown up for him.

"Anything is possible today Jonah," she reminded him one last time before he made the wish.

"Happy Birthday to You...Happy Birthday to You..." his friends sang.

His cake was festive. The birthday candles were lit and sparkled. There was stored magic within their flame. What made it magic? Was it the candles? Was it the anniversary of the birthday? Who knew, it didn't really matter to him, he knew what he had to do. It was his wish, and it would be another year around the sun, before he got another one. Anything was possible right now, but the only constraint was, he had to believe it was within the realm of possibility. He couldn't wish the moon would turn into a block of cheese, because he didn't believe that was possible.

The BobCats were there right now, helping him with the heavy burden of grief. It was his wish, to give back to them. He wanted to see his mom, and he believed if he could hear her, she was close enough he could see her, even if heaven opened up for a brief second. He wasn't sure how this was going to work out, but anything is possible, death can't be final, and his team needed this win today.

One wish, but two thoughts and two desires at once...

"Anything was possible right now," as he took a deep breath.

He blew the candles out in one swift breath.

It was done.

The blue smoke from the ten burnt candles rose towards the ceiling and with it, his unspoken birthday wish. He did his part, and now the rest was in the hands of God, or the universe. He wasn't sure who exactly handled birthday wishes, but it was now fate.

bottom of the Ninth;

The BobCats were losing...
Down by three runs at the bottom of the ninth inning, it appeared another loss was imminent. Jonah was doing his best to resist the doubt pressing in on him. The visiting Lewisburg River Cats were celebrating their third run as Jonah watched from inside of their dugout. The BobCats had given up. Their season was over, and another embarrassing shutout. Jonah closed his eyes and focused on the sound of bees buzzing near the dugout.

"It'll be your turn at bat soon Little Slugger," she seemed to say to him. No one can see a breeze when it blows, but you can sure feel it when it pushes dried leaves across the ground, and so it was when he heard his mom's voice.

The BobCat's dugout suddenly got a much needed spark when their pitcher struck out the River Cat's heavy hitter. Jake, *Spitball* Parker got his first strikeout of the season and sent the River Cat batter back to his dugout. Jonah jumped to life with the rest of his team. It was now their turn at bat, and they were only down by three runs at the moment.

"Come on guys! We can do this! We're only down by three runs!" Coach Mike Smimms yelled inside of their dugout as he fiercely clapped his hands and tried to get his dugout fired up. The BobCats could smell blood in the water, a win was suddenly possible. Spitball Parker just struck a batter out. There was a first for everything, even if it came during the final game of the season. If Spitball Parker could strike someone out, the BobCats could win this!

It would be the last chance to snatch a win from the jaws of defeat and save their team from a shutout season. It was the bottom of the ninth as Jonah watched Lefty Henderson grab a bat and take a few practice swings. Once he felt limber, he walked with laser determination towards the batter's box. Lefty was the only left handed batter on the BobCats, and suddenly found himself running for his life towards first base as his pop fly soared towards center field.

He caught a piece of the pitch and sent the baseball high towards the blinding sun.

"Run Lefty!" Coach Simms yelled from the dugout.

The BobCats screamed and yelled earnestly as little Lefty chugged towards the white bag that marked first base.

...because the River Cat's outfielder lost the ball in the sun, he dropped it. The white ball bounced off the edge of his glove and before anyone knew it, Lefty was on first base.

It was another first for the BobCats. Lefty stood proudly on first base, but still ready to run towards second base. It was the first time all season Lefty made it on base, and the BobCats needed that. There was no time to bask in the joy of getting on base, because his team was still down by three runs.

A nervous moan broke out in the BobCat dugout when their next batter swung early on his first pitch and missed.

"Strike One!" the umpire yelled in Eddie-Fastball Perkin's ear.

"Shake it off Fastball!" Coach Simms urged from his spot in the dugout.

Fastball Perkins looked at his coach, and nodded. He appeared relaxed and ready to do his part for the BobCats.

Lefty was ready, and poised to run towards second base.

Jonah pulled his ball cap down over his blue eyes and thought back in time to just a few hours ago. He could see the fading blue smoke from the candles drift towards the ceiling in the dining room. His birthday wish was sealed. Despite what he saw going on around him, there was no reason to let doubt push him around like a bully. There was a prevailing sense of hope and optimism now in the BobCat's dugout and it felt good. There was hope now for the first time this season in lot seven of the Big Valley City Park. Hope had been elusive this season for the BobCats, and now this hope felt like fire and it was about to burn hot and bright. This was starting to feel like a gift to Jonah. He was happy to see his team cheer and feel excited about the prospect of winning. Though they were still down by three runs, they all believed they could win today.

There was the familiar sound of the crack of a baseball bat as Fastball caught the next pitch just off the side of his baseball bat. He watched helplessly as the ball veered off at a sharp angle towards the bleachers.

"Foul!" the umpire yelled sternly once again in Eddie Fastball's ear.

Fastball stepped from the box and adjusted his helmet so he could see better. He took a few practice swings, and once he felt centered again, he stepped back inside of the batter's box so he could face the pitcher on the mound.

The River Cats dugout sensed the BobCats were coming out of their defeatist, humdrum attitude and didn't waste a chance to laugh at Fastball Eddie's ugly foul ball after it bounced off a car in the parking lot. Fastball ignored the jeers coming from the other dugout as he planted his feet and waited for his next pitch. The pitch came, and it was there, and so Fastball-Eddie Perkins connected with the ball. He found the sweet spot in the bat and the resounding crack from the bat hushed the jeering River Cats as his line drive sent the pitcher scurrying safely out of the way as the ball flew past the pitcher's mound as if shot from a cannon.

Both Eddie and Lefty were now safely on first and second base as Spitball Bailey Adams took her place at bat. The boys in the River Cats were acting with unsportsmanlike conduct as they made weird faces at the only girl on the BobCats. Bailey did her best to ignore their rude behavior, and didn't appreciate their unsportsmanlike showmanship, but it got the best of her when she struck out.

Tony Bianchi loaded the bases for the BobCats. Tony Bianchi's pop fly went deep into left field, but the sun did its part to blind the outfielders. The ball bounced on the ground and it allowed Lefty to make it safely to third base.

With bases loaded the coach's son was next at bat.

The Little Slugger was up after Bobby Simms.

Jonah put on his batter's helmet and took some practice swings outside of the dugout as Bobby Simms took his first pitch. As Jonah warmed up with the bat with some practice swings, some angry bees buzzed nearby. They were taking it personally that he was swinging the bat near them, but avoided him for the moment. After a few brief anxious minutes, the bees left Jonah and headed towards an overflowing trash can.

Distracted by the intrusive bees, Jonah missed in dramatic fashion as Bobby Simms swung at empty air and heard the umpire yell, "Strike Three!"

Bobby's shoulders were hanging low as he passed Jonah, but he paused long enough to smile at the Little Slugger.

"You got this Little Slugger. We believe in you," Bobby said.

Jonah smiled back. This was his destiny. Jonah might be in field seven of city park, but to him? He felt as if he were approaching his turn at bat in game seven of the World Series and he was about to possibly win it all. Jonah took a few more warm up swings and glanced at the River Cat's catcher behind him. The boy grinned mischievously at Jonah as if to remind him what was at stake.

"Easy Out!" the catcher mocked and yelled. Jonah could feel the catcher eye him up without turning around. He was wrong in his assessment of Jonah at the moment. He was trying to get inside of Jonah's head as they waited for the first pitch together.

The Little Slugger felt a wave of doubt as he took up a batter's stance. He felt so confident a moment ago, and basked in his team's hope and optimism, but now it all came down to this moment. There were two outs. He could not get out, he had to at least get on first base and drive in Lefty for their first score. He felt as if the catcher were projecting on him, and he suddenly felt crowded and intimidated by the bigger kid. Jonah started overthinking his wish.

"Was it two wishes? Did I really wish for two things, instead of one? Would it void my birthday wish?"

He was hard on himself as he stood at home plate, bat at the ready.

"I shouldn't have tried to slip two wishes in at once. I should have only made one wish, not two, you can't wish for two things at once."

It was too late. Here he was, the candles were blown out, and he'd have to wait another year before he could make another wish. The wheels of destiny were in motion as he waited for that first pitch. The air was still. He could feel the wind from the wings of bees not far away as they plucked over discarded trash.

"I'm sorry mom," Jonah thought to himself as he gripped the heavy baseball bat in his sweaty hands. *"It's all my fault. I should have only made one wish."*

"Ignore that boy behind you Little Slugger. Bobby is right, you can do this son," she said from the streets of heaven.

The bees were busy around the park today. Bumble Bees, Hornets, and Yellow Jackets were out in force, gathering nectar and picking over trash cans. The warm summer sun brought out the flowers and people, and the flowers and trash brought out foraging bees. The Yellow Jackets were particularly fond of the sticky cotton-candy and crusty lemonade cups left behind in the trash cans. Jonah's mouth felt dry, and though his nervous arms were making the bat feel heavy, he was determined to accept what happened next. He remembered the fundamentals, and would keep his eye on the ball. He would wait for the right pitch. He knew it would be there and once he saw it, he knew he would swing like Babe Ruth for the fence.

"Awww does the little boy want his mommy?" an intrusive voice suddenly said to Jonah. The catcher was still taunting Jonah. He didn't realize he'd been speaking to her out loud, loud enough for the catcher to hear, and use against him.

"Ignore him, remember today is your special day Little Slugger," she reminded. He squeezed the bat tighter. He felt as if he were standing alone on stage, all eyes on him.

"I think the little baby is crying now," the catcher said, further taunting Jonah.

Jonah's concentration was still on the catcher's verbal jabs as he wiped the tears from his eyes with his shoulder. The baseball zipped past him, well within the strike zone, a pitch he should have swung for, but the opportunity was lost as the ball landed securely inside of the catcher's mitt.

"Strike One!" the umpire yelled out in a very umpire-like fashion. The pitch was there, he should have swung and the game could be over, but he hesitated. He had to focus now. The catcher threw the baseball back to the pitcher and jeered under his catcher's mask.

Jonah was sweating. The sun felt unusually hot right now and his legs felt like limp noodles. He decided to step out of the batter's box for a moment to look at the fence in the distance. He wasn't sure how far the fence was, but he knew if he could hit the ball past that point, they would win today. It looked like a mile, and there was already one strike against him, but he had to believe the ball was destined to go over the fence. He took a couple practice swings and stood once more inside of the box next to home plate.

The next pitch came shooting towards him.

"Not this one..." his instinct said.

The ball whizzed outside of the box and landed with a boom inside of the catcher's mitt.

"Ball One!" the ump bellowed out.

"Good Eye Little Slugger!" a friendly, encouraging voice yelled. It was a welcomed relief to hear Tony Bianchi instead of the taunting catcher behind him, but it was a short respite from the annoying taunts.

"You got lucky with that one cry baby," the antagonizing voice said. The catcher threw the ball back towards his smirking, silent pitcher. It felt like it was two against one right now, but he got mentally prepared for the pitcher's next pitch.

As Jonah waited for the next pitch, an absent minded driver accidentally backed their car into a trash can not far from field seven. The bees were agitated as their treasure trove full of hot dog wrappers, popsicle sticks, and sticky soda cans went tumbling all over the ground. They buzzed menacingly near the dugout and bleachers. Onlookers swatted, and cursed the angry bees.

The unexpected drama and commotion around field seven threw Jonah off and he missed the next pitch. He swung at empty air as the ball landed securely inside of the catcher's mitt. The sound of the ball striking the leather mitt made a loud booming sound in the Little Slugger's ear. The sound was the sound of sudden looming defeat, because he now had two strikes against him. The sound of the heckling catcher added to his misery as he stepped from home plate once more to gather himself. A grand slam would win this, and though he missed her, he wanted to give his friends this gift today.

"There is no greater love than this, that a friend lays down his life for the sake of his friends," he said to himself.

His mom said it often today. The BobCats were family. The Little Slugger used the baseball bat and pointed in the direction of the fence. He was letting everyone know in faith, he was going to send the ball far out of the park, possibly as far away as the Statue of Liberty on Ferris Island.

The pitcher smirked at Jonah, but accepted the challenge. The pitcher wasn't sure why this insignificant batter was showboating like this, but he was about to teach that kid a lesson. He was going to bring the heat and see if the kid had the courage to take a swing at it. The pitcher was going to bring it. No gimmick pitch, no trickery, he would split the middle with his fast ball and see if the grandstanding kid could actually hit it. He was daring the kid to stand next to home plate as he took his stance on the pitcher's mound. The pitcher shook his head, *"No"* to the catcher's suggestions. No curveball, no change up, and no to the screwball. The catcher thumped his glove when he knew the pitcher was going to burn this kid with his fastball.

"I almost feel sorry for you kid, because of what's gonna happen next, but I'm sure your mom is out there waiting for you," the catcher said as he got ready for the next pitch.

"Yes she is," Jonah said as he stood tall in the box. The Little Slugger was confident in his faith.

The Little Slugger saw the pitch. It was there. It appeared to even slow down, despite the velocity, and defy the laws of physics, but today was Jonah's birthday, and because of faith, anything was possible.

He swung...

The bat connected with the white leather ball, with a crack so loud, the resounding noise echoed far. The ball almost split its red stitched seam as the hickory bat punished the ball. The baseball appeared as if it were blasted from the guns of a battleship as it streaked towards the blue sky. The outfielders stood helplessly and watched the baseball soar high over their heads as it traveled outside of the baseball field. It was said the ball could be seen by people on the hills somewhere deep inside of the Big Valley City Park. Joggers, peanut vendors, and couples relaxing on blankets were astounded to watch the white rocketing-baseball soar high overhead. Jonah became an instant legend within baseball circles, and the overall story joined the many other miraculous stories and moments within the park. It was said, an errant baseball cracked one of the observation windows on the replica Statue of Liberty on Ferris Island. Visitors to the island that day were caught off guard when the white ball smashed into the facade of the statue and bounced into the lake below.

No one said a word as the crowd continued to linger its gaze towards the sky in an effort to see if they could see where the ball went. It was only when Lefty reached home plate did the eyewitnesses leap to their feet. The BobCats scored their first run as Lefty chugged over home plate and into the arms of his ecstatic team. Though the River Cats were about to lose, they were in awe of Jonah as they watched him run past first base, and onward to second base. The catcher stood and took his hat and mask off, because he knew he was in the presence of greatness. The pitcher shook his head as he watched the kid run the bases. He brought his heat, but this unassuming kid smashed it so far, it disappeared. Not even Reggie Jackson could hit a ball that far. Something else was going on behind that ball. What it was, the pitcher didn't have any ideas, but it was still impressive just the same.

The swarming bees were becoming more agitated from the added, excited commotion going on around the dugouts and bleachers. The bees weren't interested in legends or baseball heroes, they were driven by instinct and perturbed by the excited energy. There was nectar to gather from flowers and discarded lemonade cups, and because of this commotion, no one noticed when Mr. Santiago was stung while tending to his food cart as he sold hotdogs to the crowd. Mr. Santiago cursed, jumped and swatted at the air. As he fought off a couple of bees with his food tongs, he rubbed his swollen neck.

While Mr. Santiago fought off the bees, Fastball-Eddie jumped triumphantly on home plate to score the next run for the BobCats.

Tony Bianchi was the next BobCat to cross home plate and officially tie up the game with the River Cats. He jumped up and down as he tossed his batter's helmet into the air and hugged his team. The longest losing streak in little league baseball circles was about to end today, and he was thrilled to be a part of the winning team.

Winning was sweet! The team realized and wanted to savor and relish the moment as they waited for the Little Slugger to cross home plate and put this win into the history books.

Jonah rounded third base. He did it! His heart swelled from joy as he ran towards home. He put his friends ahead of himself, and what he wanted, so they could have this moment. They were ready to pile on him from excitement and the thrill of victory. The Little Slugger, now known as the Sultan of Swing from Big Valley crossed home plate. It was done. The BobCats were the victor as they engulfed Jonah at home plate.

Mr. Santiago managed to find some bee ointment in a first aid kit as he warned his customers to be watchful of the agitated bees. As Mr. Santiago warned people near the ballfield of the bees, no one noticed Jonah wince in pain as he felt a dreadful, painful sting on the back of his neck. The River Cats lined up with a fresh demonstration of good sportsmanship to congratulate the BobCats for their stunning victory as Jonah felt his throat swell shut. Jonah and his dad were not aware that the Little Slugger was deadly allergic to bee stings. They were simply not prepared for what was happening as Jonah felt an invisible hand squeezing his throat shut.

He wanted to celebrate, but he felt as if he were falling into a fog. As Jonah fell inside of the disorienting fog, he heard someone call for him.

The crowd was thinning out, falling away. He was not aware of a sudden frantic rush to help him as his body hit the ground, unresponsive. As bystanders tried to render first aid to Jonah, he reached for his mom and walked away from home plate.

His wish did come true. He didn't know how the details would play out exactly, but the BobCats won, and now his mom was holding his hand. He wasn't sure if this counted as two wishes, but it didn't matter, because none of it really mattered now. He wanted to go with her, and not come back. Jonah's mom could never really return to spend his birthday with him, but he could go to her and visit her within this new realm. Jonah was now within the *in-between* space. It was the invisible space where life, and death meet, and sometimes someone goes there for a moment before they come back. Judy Martz could never back from where she went, because she arrived at her final resting place, but she could meet her boy in the middle space, and spend a little time with him today as the paramedics worked on him.

The EMS feverishly worked on Jonah to restore his breathing and bring him back from that twilight space. Jonah was at total peace, and had what he wanted. He never wanted to go back without his mom.

together;

"*Happy Birthday Little Slugger!*" He could hear his mom yell from outside of the park. He could hear her with his actual ear, instead of hearing her voice from within his memory.

There she was; waving and smiling.

Though he'd smashed the baseball out of the park, and won the game with a grandslam, that was only part of what he wanted for his birthday. The swirling fog appeared to burn away and his mom became clearer the further he went from his body. She was standing on the other side of the outfield fence. He started running towards his mom, and wasted no time climbing the fence to be with her.

"We're losing him!" a bystander yelled as they continued to administer first aid.

Jonah was unaware of the approaching ambulance. He was lost in his mom's comforting arms as they loaded his unresponsive body into the back of the ambulance. His mom's face beamed, her eyes sparkled, and her whimsical freckled face was full of vibrant life. She was no longer suffering from pain and the illness that took her away.

"Oh Little Slugger, I've missed you so much," she said as she squeezed her son tightly. Jonah never wanted to go back to the other side. He wanted to go with his mom.

From where he stood, he didn't notice the ambulance leaving for the hospital with him, because *he* was inside of the in-between. His body was an empty container as it was driven to the hospital by the ambulance. The in-between was the valley and Jonah was standing under the shadows of two distinct places. He could sense life where he had come from, and remembered the direction to go if he had to return to the other side, but on the other side of the valley, the side where his mom came from, appeared much too far for him to go, unless he let go and never came back. So it was inside of the in-between space. It was a journey to cross over from the different sides of life.

"You can't stay over here for very long Jonah, your place is over there for now," his mom urged.

Despite her insistence, there was no hurry for him to go back to the other side. No sense of urgency on his part. This was what he wished for and it was his special day. How could anyone expect him to go back right now? He had so many questions, but all he wanted to do was be close to her.

It was still summer inside of the in-between. It was pleasantly warm as kids swam in the pool and kites shared the blue sky with lazy clouds. No one noticed as Jonah and his mom walked the paths around the park. They were translucent and unnoticed by those who remained where Jonah belonged.

They eventually made their way to the small Statue of Liberty. Like most days, it was packed with curious visitors as they passed unnoticed. Many of the out of town visitors marveled at the peculiar *must-see* attraction. They came from far and wide to see the scaled down, infamous miniature statue.

Jonah and his mom found themselves inside of Lady Liberty and despite the lines of tourists, they remained unseen. Jonah and his mom were occupying two seperate places, but within the space. They were inside of the Statue of Liberty which was positioned on Ferris Island, inside of the park, but they were also inside of the in-between space. Two defining borders, but invisible unless you were traveling to the other side.

Though the statue was only half the size of the actual Statue of Liberty, it was listed in many travel brochures. The park was the hub of activity year around, and today was no exception as the Little Slugger and his mom stood atop of the statue's crown and watched the life going on inside of the park below. Though his body was somewhere else, Jonah was taking in the warmth of the radiant sun and the closeness of his mom. The sun felt brighter, more vibrant, and oddly closer in the in-between.

His mom told him, "It feels this way, because here we're closer to heaven. The glory of heaven is so much, we can feel it here in the in-between. It's like climbing a hill, and before you reach the top, you can begin to see the other side."

No one could see the reunion taking place inside of the infamous statue. Jonah felt as if he were flying high above the rolling mountains surrounding Big

Valley, and well above the reach of the familiar Savage Tire Plant smokestacks. He felt as if he were in a dream, but as those images faded, and the sense he was flying, he found himself sitting on a park bench, next to Ferris Lake, next to his mom. He couldn't remember walking there, but here in the in-between the normal laws of nature didn't seem to apply. Jonah could now see what appeared to be two suns in the blue sky. One of the two suns dwarfed the other sun as Jonah realized the biggest sun was the physical boundary of heaven. Heaven's gates were within sight of the Little Slugger right now the longer he spent inside of the in-between.

Jonah felt sleepy. He wanted to take a nap in his mom's lap and couldn't resist the urge to lay down and sleep. As he laid down in her familiar lap, she stroked his hair with a gentle, nurturing hand. They still occupied one space, but from another space as they watched children sail small model sailboats across the calm, lake water. It was disorienting to Jonah and despite his reunion and the majesty of heaven, just over the next hill, it was hard for him to get his bearings. Life suddenly felt like the fragile wooden, model sailboats gliding over the water. He didn't like the in-between space and wanted to go with his mom towards the light of heaven.

"I know this place feels like an upside down moon-bounce to you right now. You can feel the pull from the other side, the side where you belong Jonah, now is not your time to come home with me. Not today, nor is this place meant for anyone to remain within, but it was the only way we could see each other. Your faith was honored today Little Slugger, you'll go back to your dad, back to your friends, you gave them a scare, but you'll be okay son," his mom whispered gently as she continued to gently stroke his hair.

Though his memories felt like they were coming from across a distant ocean on the wings of an ocean soaring bird, he could remember his life on the other side. He could remember the grand slam. He remembered his dad and the friends he made from the BobCats. The longer he remained in the in-between, the less he remembered about his life on the other side, a place he traveled from just a few minutes before. Though it was noon, and there appeared to be two warm suns in the sky, Jonah felt so tired and wanted his mom to tuck him in. He felt safe in her lap, and the pain of missing her was not something he remembered right now.

Though the nurses and doctors were working to bring Jonah back from the other side, back from the in-between, he resisted the current pulling back to where he belonged.

He still had questions for her, and his mother seemed to know what those questions were.

"When we get to heaven Little Slugger, we're never told why we were taken when we were. Faith brought us together today, and by faith we accept the Father's will and destiny for his creation. You don't have your sea legs, and time feels funny to you, because you weren't meant to go past this place, nor remain here. One year over here, feels like a second over there Jonah. We have no need for time anymore, and one day, you'll see what I mean, but this is why you have to go back."

"I don't want to go back over there, please I want to stay here with you."

"We can't stay here Jonah," his mom said in a serious tone. "This valley, it wasn't meant for us to live in. This valley belongs to death. We only pass through this place as we head towards home, or the other place. This valley coexists, side by side with where you live, and where my home is now. Sometimes souls come here and visit briefly, and go back, and that's what happened to you son. I know it feels like you've been here all day, but you haven't. You've been with me in the park, for only a few minutes."

The Little Slugger continued to fight the crushing need to close his eyes and sleep, because if he did and let go, the tide would yank him back to where his body was. The other side was pulling him back, away from her.

"It's not your time to go with me over there. It's time for you to go and live your life, and you will and that makes me happy. I am so proud of you today, you were brave to take that swing for your friends today, and be willing to sacrifice yourself for them."

He managed to open his eyes, enough to study her face one last time. Her face looked at peace. Her eyes were full of joy, and understanding. There were no more tears, no more ravages of the disease that took her life. Though he knew he was sad she was gone, he knew she was healed from the illness, and he would be with her again one day. He knew from her perspective, Jonah would come back to live with her in heaven in a short amount of time, because of how time felt on this side.

"You have many more birthdays ahead of you Jonah," she whispered as she kissed his forehead.

They were separated once again by the invisible boundary between life, and life after. Separated from the place Jonah lives, and where his mom lives. It was an immeasurable expanse, a place where souls pass as they make their way to their final destination and resting place.

She remained with him until he was safely back home in his body, before she returned to the place that looked like a bright shining star on a hill, and as she left the in-between space for home, she knew she would see her little boy again when his time came to join her, and it would be a marvelous homecoming when that time came.

Jonah saw a white light rushing towards him as if he were passing through a narrow tunnel. The light got brighter, brighter, and he felt the weight of gravity on his body. He could hear what sounded like an organized chaos going on around him.

"Welcome back son! We have a pulse now, it's weak, but we have one!" a doctor yelled to others standing near Jonah. Jonah passed through the fog of the in-between and returned to his body, now inside of an emergency room.

He opened his eyes, but wasn't able to speak, because of the tube in his mouth. Jonah felt disoriented, and couldn't remember how he got here. Unfamiliar faces were looking down at him. They were dressed in lab coats, and scrub uniforms.

"We thought we lost him for good, it was close, but he's stable for the moment. Where is his father?" a man in a lab coat asked.

"Doctor Edwards, the boy's father is outside in the waiting room."

"Is there a mom?" Doctor Edwards asked.

"No, from what the father told me, his mom passed several years ago."

"Thank you nurse," Doctor Edwards grimaced and looked back down at his young patient he just revived. "Poor kid, he almost went to her today, but it wasn't his time." He listened to Jonah's breathing again with a stethoscope for another minute. "Jonah, my name is Doctor Edwards. Son, you're in the hospital, because you were stung by a bee, and apparently you're deathly allergic to bees. We'll get the tube out of your mouth in a few minutes, I just want to make sure you're totally free of danger again before we remove the tube that's helping you breathe."

Jonah looked blankly at Doctor Edwards. He remembered coming from somewhere, but doesn't remember where he came from. Jonah doesn't remember the bee sting, or his trip to the hospital, but he had an intuitive sense, he'd been somewhere.

A nurse squeezed his hand gently. She smiled at him. He felt as if he were waking up from a deep sleep. He felt as if he were waking up from a dream about his mom, a dream he could no longer remember. Doctor Edwards didn't have to tell him about his brush with death, because he knew he'd left this place, and went on a journey, but unlike him, his mother went further in her journey than he did, because he came back. He didn't understand it fully to talk about with anyone, it was just something he understood.

what happened next;

Years after this experience, Jonah Martz did confide in me what happened that day in the park. We remained friends until we graduated college and life took us in different directions. We both attended the same university, same frat brotherhood, and one night he opened up after we'd had a few drinks.

I understood today, after hearing the news of his passing, he passed on through the in-between space. He didn't come back this time like he did when we were ten years old. Much has been written about near death experiences, and Jonah had one when we were kids.

As a precaution in the years that followed his near fatal reaction to the bee, he would always carry an epipen, especially during the spring and summer months. Though he had many more birthdays, Jonah never wished he could have one more day with his mom. When he was an adult, Jonah read books, and attended seminars, often hosted by doctors who studied the field of near death experiences. The details always felt vague, opaque, as if he were trying to look through a dark glass, hoping to get a glimpse to the other side.

From that day onward, he knew his mom was indeed close to him. She was at peace, healed from the illness and full of new life. As the years came and went, Jonah lost his grandparents, dad, and some childhood friends. He knew there was an "in-between" frontier, a place that separates life here, and life in heaven. It was the place where people did experience momentary death, down in the valley, before they went up to the star-like city on the hill.

My friend Jonah Martz, had a life to live and grew into an adult over time. He, like most of us, lost his childlike faith, the faith it took to believe in the power of wishes. Eventually life chipped away at his faith, and he became cynical. He lost the desire to just skip rocks with his friends across the lake. He no longer believed in birthday wishes, just before he blew out the candles.

Remember the Savage Tire Plant? Sadly, the plant folded back in 1988. A competitor bought the company, just to shutter the plant and lay off most of our city. Big Valley fell into a deep economic recession after that, but that was until another miracle happened in the city park, and rescued the city from falling off a cliff, and into an abyss of hopelessness. The Big Valley Badgers, our local high school football team, managed to rally the city together during those dark days, but that's another story, for another time. There's a lot of magic inside of that park, because they say it's enchanted. I'm not sure, but it's a neat, whimsical place to visit if you're ever near Big Valley. If you do find your way out there and take a moment to visit the park, be sure to go see the miniaturized Statue of Liberty, you won't be disappointed. I promise.

They say God answers our prayers. Maybe birthday wishes are simple prayers, expressions of faith. I've heard it said, we should all come in faith to God, because he hears us. I am sad for those kids today, because it seems they age faster than we did. From what I've observed and experienced from my kids and their friends, they appear to embrace cynicism and doubt faster than we did when we became adults. We were so quick to want to become adults, we regretted this when we actually became adults. I used to believe in Santa, so did my kids, but not anymore, because now Christmas has lost its magic and become an idea corporations use to market consumer merchandise. Perhaps Santa is real, and remains in the North Pole, because we no longer believe.

Contact

jlatkisson@gmail.com

———— ⟳ ————

Other Titles by this Author

Fiction

-The Little Slugger-
-Fly Little Bird; Come Fly Me Home-
-Stop the Nukes My Stories are On!!-
-Roller Derby Apocalypse-

Titles Written Under My Pen Name

*Denotes Pen Name
-When an Angel Intervenes-
Christian Price
-Big Valley Football: The Legend of The Badgers-
Christian Price

Non Fiction

-A Change of Heart: From Suicide to Life-
-Living Beyond Suicide's Moment After-